Other Works By Brandon G. Kroupa

The Seventh Year

The Snowball Effect

SAINT NICK

A Novel

Brandon G. Kroupa

Chapbook Press

Schuler Books
2660 28th Street SE
Grand Rapids, MI 49512
(616) 942-7330
www.schulerbooks.com

Saint Nick

ISBN 13: 9781943359202

Library of Congress Control Number: 2015955690

Printed in the United States by Chapbook Press.

A Note To You The Reader…

Bronner's CHRISTmas Wonderland, the Bavarian Inn, Frankenmuth, Michigan, the Village of Zell (located in the Bavarian Forest in Germany), and Parish Church in Zell are actual places that are depicted within this story.

Artistic liberties were taken in the descriptions of Zell and Parish Church in order to fit my story.

With regards to Bronner's CHRISTmas Wonderland, the Bavarian Inn, and Frankenmuth, Michigan, their descriptions are based upon first hand knowledge from visiting them on a regular basis over the years.

It is important to note that Bronner's CHRISTmas Wonderland and the Bavarian Inn update their décor from time to time. So should you ever visit them, and I highly recommend that you do, their interiors may look a bit different than described herein.

"Santa's Christmas Prayer"

On Christmas Eve the other night
I saw the most amazing sight,
For there beneath the Christmas Tree
Was Santa kneeling on his knee.

His countenance was different than
That all-familiar, jolly grin;
His head was bowed, with hand to breast
And slightly tucked into his vest.

For there in a nativity was
Jesus and His family,
And as I heard him start to pray
I listened close to what he'd say.

"Lord, You know that You're the reason
I take pleasure in this season.
I don't want to take Your place,
But just reflect your wondrous grace.

I hope You'll help them understand
I'm just an ordinary man,
Who found a way to do Your will
By finding kids with needs to fill.

But all those centuries ago,
There was no way for me to know
That they would make so much of me,
And all the gifts beneath the tree.

They think I have some hidden power
Granted at the midnight hour,
But it is my love for You
Inspiring the things I do.

And so when they begin to open
Gifts for which they have been hoping.
May they give You all the glory,
For You're the One True Christmas Story."

- Alda Monteschio

Our Lord

At

Zell

"The Spirit of Christmas is ageless, irresistible and knows no barriers. It reaches out to add a glow to the humblest of homes and the stateliest of mansions. It catches up saint and sinner alike in its warm embrace. It is the season to be jolly — but to be silent and prayerful as well."

- President Gerald R. Ford
from his Christmas Message
12/24/75

Chapter 1

In the southeastern corner of Germany, bordered by the countries of Austria, Czech Republic and Switzerland, rests the state of Bavaria. Rich in culture and history, Bavaria is one of the oldest states in Europe, dating back to the seventeenth century. Some areas within Bavaria date back even further.

One area, the Bavarian Forest, is a remnant from the Hercynian Forest when the land was known as Germania during the time of the Roman Empire. Deep within this beautiful enchanted forest lay many towns and villages. One built within a large clearing in the forest is the beautifully simple village of Zell.

As dusk begins to settle on the village, a light snow begins to fall. The soft, light flakes land delicately upon the rooftops. They begin to glisten as the last rays of the sun caress them before it disappears below the treetops of the forest. No rooftop in the village glistens more radiantly than that of the Parish Church. Built in the center of the village (a common practice throughout Europe) the church glows as a beacon of light for all to find their way. Even as the darkness of night begins to take hold of the village and the luminance from the rooftops begins to wane, the rooftop of Parish Church remains as radiant as before. How this is possible can only be described as divine.

The cold, Gothic-style church has uncanny warmth about it. As the main door opens, an elderly gentleman with a thick, diminutive, gray beard; mustache; and short, slightly curly matching hair emerges. He gazes over the village with a face that would appear to look weathered and stern, but is truly soft and majestic. Adjusting his overcoat and mittens, he turns to the priest who followed him out, "Thank you so much for the coffee and stimulating conversation, Father Green. It has been quite some time since I have had the pleasure of either. It was much appreciated."

"You are most welcome, my son" replies Father Green. "But I have not had the pleasure of knowing your name."

"That is because I did not offer it, Father." The Elderly Gentleman pauses for a moment as a thought crosses his mind. Giving Father Green a warm look, he explains "I have many names, Father. You of all people should know this."

Father Green stands confused at the Elderly Gentleman's words. As he thinks of what to say, the Elderly Gentleman says to him, "A famous author once said, I can't recall at the moment who, but he said that we are all travelers in the wilderness of this world, and the best that we can find in our travels is an honest friend."

Instantly recognizing the quote, Father Green responds "So says Robert Louis Stevenson."

"Ah, yes! That is it!" exclaims the Elderly Gentleman. "Thank you for refreshing my memory."

"You're welcome" says Father Green. "I have to ask, if I may, have you found this honest friend in your travels?"

"It is funny you should mention it. As a matter of fact, I have. That is what brings me to your beautiful village. I am told that he lives nearby."

"Perhaps I can be of some assistance to you, my son. I know many of the people in the village."

"That would be most kind of you" replies the Elderly Gentleman. "His name is Nicholas."

"Nicholas?" questions Father Green. "Not much to go on. I know many people named Nicholas. Do you happen to know his last name by chance?"

"No last name, just Nicholas."

"That's really not much to go on" Father Green admits. Thinking for a moment he asks "What does Nicholas look like?"

"Like St. Nicholas" replies the Elderly Gentleman.

"Are you referring to the Christian Saint or Santa Claus?"

"Both actually."

Father Green is completely dumbfounded at the Elderly Gentleman's response. Putting his hand to his chin, he begins to contemplate and decipher the man's comment. Then it comes to him. "You must mean Ol' Nick! He lives in a cabin deep inside the forest just north of here. I see him every Sunday, even in the worst of weather. How he manages to get here through some of that, I will never know."

"If you know him as I do, Father, you know that he is a very dedicated man. Thank you, my son. You have been most helpful and very kind." He places his hand upon Father Green's shoulder and in a very reassuring manner tells him "Peace be with you my son."

"And with you" replies Father Green.

With that the Elderly Gentleman turns and makes his way down the street heading north towards the forest. Father Green watches him walk away. He turns to head back inside the church and suddenly pauses. Something the Elderly Gentleman said earlier in their conversation strikes a resonating chord. He quickly turns to find that the Elderly Gentleman has vanished. There is no trace of him, not even a footprint left behind in the freshly fallen snow.

Pondering this, the answer becomes obviously clear to Father Green. Smiling, he walks back inside the church and looks out toward the street.

As he closes the door, he begins to quote aloud, "Be not forgetful to entertain strangers for thereby some have entertained angels unaware. Hebrews 13:2."

Nicholas's

Task

"Oh, Christmas isn't just a day, it's a frame of mind…and that's what's been changing. That's why I'm glad I'm here, maybe I can do something about it."

- *Edmund Gwenn, as Kris Kringle*
*from "**A Miracle On 34th Street**"*
(1947)

Chapter 2

The Elderly Gentleman makes his way through the forest just north of Zell. Even though the woodlands are dimly lit, this doesn't seem to faze him at all. With a simple motion of his hand, the stars and the moon instantly brighten giving him more than enough light to find his way. It begins to snow, adding a most beautiful pattern to the already pristine blanket upon the ground.

Stopping for a moment, he looks at the outfit he is wearing. Feeling out of place with a quick snap of his fingers, the overcoat he is wearing lengthens to become a fur lined cape with a hood. Reaching down he picks up a broken branch. While grasping it in his hand the branch suddenly comes to life. The dead pieces fall off and the branch begins to morph into a long, simple yet beautiful crozier. Satisfied with his efforts the Elderly Gentleman pulls the hood of his cape over his head and continues his trek through the forest.

As he traverses through the trees, the forest around him becomes much more vibrant and full of life. It is as though winter's grip isn't even present. Taking his time he admires and contemplates all the great beauty that this land has to offer. Walking for hours is nothing more than mere minutes to Him. Lost in his thoughts he wanders into a clearing that appears out of nowhere. At the far end of the clearing is the cottage that he seeks, one that is unlike any other in the area.

Built out of thick logs it is fashioned in distinct Bavarian architecture. In the light of the moon, its green roof glistens with drifts of snow piled in its distinct corners. The front window of the cottage is draped with fresh pine garland that has bright bows positioned in between each string. A small flower box below the window contains three small Christmas trees decorated with many small colored bulbs. When the light of the moon strikes them, they give the appearance of being lit with actual lights. A warm glow emanating from inside the cottage enhances this effect.

A large landing built off from one of the upper level rooms of the cottage is its most distinctive feature. Unlike most landings, this one was built in a perfect circle around the trunk of a large conifer growing next to the cottage. The railings surrounding the landing are carved with the faces of forest animals and religious symbols. These carvings are so elaborate, so detailed, and so perfect, only a master craftsman could have done the work.

Standing on the landing underneath a low hanging bow of the conifer is Nicholas. Nicholas is very familiar in appearance but not dressed as one would commonly picture him. He wears a yellow shirt and brown lederhosen held up by traditional Bavarian suspenders. Thick wool socks come up to his knees out of black leather boots. They look dressy but are in fact made specifically for the snow. A long flowing green coat hangs open exposing its red fabric lining trimmed in gold. Finally, the hat he wears is a traditional velvet Bavarian with a feather coming out of the side.

Leaning onto the railing, Nicholas observes his surroundings and notices that things are becoming more vibrant. Sensing something is about he leans over the railing to peer into the distance. It takes him only a second to spy the cloaked Elderly Gentleman at the edge of the clearing, heading towards the cottage. Nicholas gestures to him with a wave.

The Elderly Gentlemen observing this, pauses for a moment to return the gesture. He then continues his trek toward the cottage as he watches Nicholas walk back into the cottage.

As Nicholas moves inside from the landing, he walks down a small hallway then down a small spiral staircase to the main floor. Passing through the living room one notices that it is very simple and modest. A great fireplace is lit with a beautifully stoked fire. Two meticulously carved, nicely padded chairs sit in front of it.

Above the mantle are four impressive oil paintings arranged in staggered fashion. The first is that of the patron Saint Nicholas dressed in traditional ecclesiastic garb, wearing a miter, and holding a crozier. The next painting depicts Jesus, kneeling at a log praying, as a ray of light from the heavens above shine down upon him. The third is a Norman Rockwell of Santa Claus. The fourth and final is an interpretation of God similar to that of Da Vinci's painting on the ceiling of the Sistine Chapel.

Walking into the breezeway, Nicholas takes off his hat. With a twist of his wrist he tosses it towards a shelf where it lands perfectly in between a Bishop's Miter and a Santa hat. Nicholas waits for only a moment before a knock comes upon the door. Grasping the knob he opens it to see the Elderly Gentleman standing there. How he managed to get to the cottage so quickly from where he was (and not even be winded) is nothing short of a miracle.

The Elderly Gentleman reveals himself as he lowers his hood. Looking directly at Nicholas he states, "I am a stranger in this land. I seek rest and perhaps a beverage."

"My door is always open to the traveler." Nicholas gestures him in, "And you, Lord, are always welcome in my home."

"Something these days is becoming more and more scarce" the Lord replies.

"Well, Jesus said "*Ask and you shall receive, seek and you shall find, knock and the door will be opened to you*" states Nicholas.

To which the Lord replies "For everyone who asks, receives; he who seeks, finds; and to him whom knocks, the door shall be opened. Wise man, my son. Who do you think he learned it from?"

"That question is rhetorical, Lord, as it was you. Something that more people these days should do" comments Nicholas.

"Agreed" says the Lord. Nicholas motions him inside and towards the living room to one of the chairs in front of the fire. Closing the door he turns to the Lord and asks "What can I offer you?"

"A nice cup of cocoa would be very pleasing, if you have it."

"I do, as a matter of fact. Please, make yourself at home" Nicholas tells him as he goes into the kitchen to grant the Lord's request.

The Lord stands in front of the fireplace admiring the painting above the mantel. He tells Nicholas, "These pictures are very simple, yet very accurate. Except the one of me…it looks nothing like me at all!"

Nicholas coming out of the kitchen, holding two mugs in his hands, explains "Each man has a different perspective of his vision of you, Lord."

"This is very true" taking one of the mugs from Nicholas. "I very much like this one of you, the way you looked so long ago" referring to the picture of the patron Saint Nicholas.

"Though I may not look like that now, I still hold those beliefs I did so long ago, Lord. It is not what the man looks like but who he is inside which matters."

"So true and well spoken, Nicholas" comments the Lord.

Nicholas motions to the Lord to make himself comfortable. Nicholas stands until the Lord has seated himself and waits for him to return the gesture to join him. Sitting down, Nicholas takes a sip of his beverage and asks "What service can I do for you, Lord?"

"Now why would you think I am here to ask something of you?"

"Though you come for visits often, it is the look upon your face that tells me it is so."

"I can't fool you, Nicholas. What brings me is there has been a loss of the true meaning of Christmas. Christmas has become too commercialized. The youth these days don't even believe in Santa Claus let alone what the season is truly about" says the Lord.

"I, of course, am at your service. What would you have me do, Lord?" asks Nicholas.

"Go seek out a child of 8. Prove to the child you are Santa and reaffirm what the season is truly about. The child in turn will start the mend and put Christmas back as it should be."

"Where am I to find this child?"

"Travel to the United States, to a small town in the state of Michigan named Frankenmuth. It is nicknamed "Michigan's Little Bavaria". There you will find a place called Bronner's CHRISTmas Wonderland. It was built by a man, who now resides in my kingdom, named Wally Bronner. Wally was very devoted man who held Christ in his heart and knew that He was the center of Christmas. Wally lived and expressed this fact 365 days a year without fail. The meaning of his store's motto says it all, that Christmas is the celebration of Christ's birth. I can't think of a better place to prove such a thing."

"I agree. I will use all of the gifts you have bestowed upon me in order to do so" replies Nicholas.

"I knew you would, Nicholas. It is always polite to ask though" says the Lord.

Nicholas nods to acknowledge this.

The Lord and Nicholas sit in silence and stare into the fire. With a small motion of his hand, the Lord reveals to Nicholas the snowy Winter Wonderland of Michigan and a car making its way into Frankenmuth towards Bronner's CHRISTmas Wonderland.

Arriving

At Bronner's

"Never worry about the size of your Christmas Tree. In the eyes of children, they are all 30 feet tall."

- Larry Wilde

Chapter 3

1

Harrison Fahs could see the old Farmer's Antique Mall in the distance as he drove down Highway M-54. He knew that just up ahead was the junction for M-83 and the last leg of the family's trip to Frankenmuth. The two and a half hour drive from their home in Reed City had gone by rather quickly. The roads along the way had been wet but clear, and the sky couldn't decide whether to be sunny or overcast. And although they encountered an occasional snow squall along the way, it had been smooth sailing since they left home. That was saying quite a bit since the weather in Michigan could be very unpredictable, especially in early December.

As he approached the light at the junction for his turn, Harrison could remember his grandparents, even his parents for that matter, telling him while he was growing up that "*If you don't like the weather in Michigan, wait five minutes and it'll change.*"

What a true statement this turned out to be as a light, fluffy snow began to fall just after he made the turn onto M-83. All Harrison could do was shake his head and chuckle that this happened at the precise moment he'd been thinking about it.

His chuckle drew the attention of his wife, Audrey, who had been gazing out the passenger's window while taking in the beauty of the snow covered farm fields of corn and soybeans. "What's got your funny bone going?" she asked.

"Just thinking about how just a second ago it was sunny and clear, and now its snowing like sixty" replied Harrison.

"Only in Michigan my parents would say" Audrey quips back without missing a beat.

"I was thinking that exact same thing!" Harrison tells her as he takes a quick glimpse into the rear view mirror to see his daughter Heather still zonked out in the back seat. With a look of triumph on his face he states proudly "At least we made the trip over without any fussing this time around."

"Don't get too cocky over there Harry and go jinxing yourself" warns Audrey, "We're not there yet."

Before Harrison can get his own two cents in edgewise, he is cut off by an earsplitting voice from the backseat shrieking out those four little words every parent on the face of the planet dreads hearing on any long trip "*ARE WE THERE YET?!*"

Harrison quickly looks over at Audrey telling her "Don't say it!"

"Oh, but I am going to say it" she tells him with a devilish grin on her face. "I told you so!"

"I know, I know" agrees Harrison reluctantly.

"Dad, are we there yet?!" asks Heather again this time even more impatient.

Hesitating to answer the question Harrison catches a glimpse of a sign that reads...

FRANKENMUTH   4.5 MILES

"Yes, honey we are almost there" he tells her confidently, "We should be there in roughly five minutes."

Heather smiled with great anticipation about being just minutes away. This was her very first trip to Frankenmuth and Bronner's. Her parents had come here a number of times over the years. When they did, she usually spent the weekend with her Grandma And Grandpa Fahs in Traverse City. This time though was different. This time she got to come along, and she was more than excited. Staring out the window, she imagined how it would look compared to what she had been told by her parents. It wouldn't be long now.

Her concentration was precipitously broken as she spied a small church they were coming upon. In the church's front lawn, in the snow, were very large letters spelling out the word HOPE. It wasn't the church or the oversized word that drew her attention but a figure standing at the end of the word. That figure was of Nicholas dressed as Santa Claus.

"SANTA! LOOK ITS SANTA!" she yells enthusiastically, pointing at the spot where she saw him.

Harrison and Audrey take a quick look back but see nothing but a church and the word HOPE in front. No Santa Claus standing there. "There's no one there, Heather" Audrey tells her.

"But I saw him! He was there just a second ago" she tells them as she frantically looks back to see no one there.

"You're just so excited right now, Heather, your mind is playing tricks on you, that's all" explains Harrison.

"I know I saw him! I know I did!" Heather assures her parents.

"We know you want to see Santa, Heather. You will be able to see him when we get to Bronner's" Audrey tells her.

"Cool! I have lots to ask him for this year. We can go and see him first thing right?"

"We'll see" says Harrison explaining 'There are other things to see at Bronner's besides Santa Claus."

"Like Rudolph, Dad?"

"Rudolph?"

"Yea, see him there" she says pointing to a deer crossing sign they are passing. Someone had purposely placed a "red nose" on the deer.

"*That's cute*" Harrison thought. "I suppose that is possible as well" he tells her.

"So are we there yet?" asks Heather in an urgent tone adding the explanation "I have to go potty."

"Yes, we are" Audrey assures her as she taps Harrison on the arm, motioning him to take a look out the window. Looking out, he spots the Old Iron Bridge at Tiny's Farm and knows their destination lies ahead around the next bend.

2

Rounding the bend, Harrison sees the Silent Night Chapel that lies just in front of Bronner's parking lot. Clearing the corner and heading into the main stretch, he tells Heather "There it is" and motions for her to look out the window.

Heather quickly turns, plastering her face to the car's window and gazes out at the wonder that is Bronner's CHRISTmas Wonderland. The huge store spans the size of more than 1.5 football fields and is completely surrounded by holiday decorations throughout the grounds. Snowmen, Santa's, elves, Christmas trees, Nativity's, oversized ornaments, and arctic animals are just a few of the things Heather sees as they pass by. There are so many other things she sees that she is very overwhelmed at the sight of it all.

What crushes her is the vast "millions" of cars in the store's parking lot. "Are they all here to see Santa, too?" she asks. "'Cause if they are I'll be waiting forever to see him!"

"Maybe" Audrey responds. "But I don't think so" she reassures her. In an attempt to take her mind off Santa for a moment, Audrey points out all the pretty lights that are on the grounds. They make the turn onto 25 Christmas Lane.

"Wish it was darker so we could see all the pretty lights lit up, Mommy" Heather tells her.

"Well, perhaps later when we leave it will be dark enough for them to be on, and we can see them then" explains Audrey.

Audrey no more than finishes telling Heather this, when out of the blue, day turns into night. As it does, it triggers the sensors on the lights around the grounds causing them to instantly turn on and illuminate the grounds.

"WOW!" exclaims Heather in amazement as she takes in all the beautiful lights.

"Wow is one way to put it" adds Harrison. "Have you ever seen anything like that happen before?"

"No" responds Audrey. "This is rather strange" she adds.

"Second time today this has happened" says Harrison referring to earlier when it went from sunny and clear, to snowing all of a sudden.

Turning into the lot, Harrison scans for a place to park. After a couple of minutes driving up and down multiple aisles, he finally finds a spot, which seems like Outer Mongolia in comparison to the store.

The family puts on their jackets and exits the vehicle. Harrison no sooner shuts his door when he hears Audrey tell him "Ah-hem. Excuse me, but I think you need to pay up there pal."

Rolling his eyes, Harrison pulls out his wallet from his back pocket. Opening it, he thumbs through the bills and retracts a $1 bill; then closes it before replacing it in his pocket. With the dollar in hand, he walks around the car and grudgingly holds it out. "I know" he tells her "Don't say it."

"Not a word, but what did I tell you?" she taunts.

"You told me so. I know. Listen to me, you said. I didn't and it cost me." Harrison admits.

"Exactly!" exclaims Audrey snatching the dollar out of his hand, shaking her head and smiling as she does. "Thank you-u-u-u-u!"

Heather laughs asking "Where's my dollar, Daddy? Why does Mommy get one and not me?"

"Mom gets one because your Dad bet her that you wouldn't wake up till *after* we got here" explains Harrison. "You woke up before we did, and your Dad didn't want to listen. Besides, I thought you had to use the bathroom?" he adds, trying to change the subject.

"Not so much anymore. Can we go inside? I want to see Santa!"

"Okay then. Let's get this show on the road" he tells her.

They begin their trek across the parking lot toward the store, stopping to take pictures of the 20 foot snowman and the 70 foot iconic Bronner's Santa. As they head up the main sidewalk toward the West Entrance of the store, they do their best not to bump into all the hustling and bustling shoppers, a sure telltale sign of the Christmas Season.

Finally reaching the doors, the family stops. Harrison looks over at Audrey and smiles, then looks down at Heather and asks "You ready?"

"Yup!" she answers.

"Then in we go!" Harrison responds.

They walk together, triggering the West Entrance doors to open. As they enter, a rush of warm, Christmas-smelling air washes over them.

Waiting

For

Santa

"Even as an adult I find it difficult to sleep on Christmas Eve. Yuletide excitement is potent caffeine, no matter your age."

- Carrie Latet

Chapter 4

1

Entering the store, Heather is instantly drawn to one whopper of a Christmas tree. Just barely grazing the lobby ceiling, it's decorated to the hilt with oversized peppermint candies, gingerbread men, bows of rich, dark metallic colors, and is lighted from top to bottom with more than a thousand lights. She is in awe at the sight, never seeing a Christmas tree of this magnitude before.

What ensnares her attention further is the Santa Claus situated in the corner of the entrance door. With the look of fine porcelain, the Santa holds a great big sack in front of him, giving the impression he is delivering presents under the tree to all those good little children. Walking closer to it, Heather realizes that it is as tall as she is. She studies the Santa's face intently, giving it a cheery smile. Although it already had a bright, friendly, jolly ol' smile upon its face, Heather was suddenly taken aback when the Santa appeared to return her smile.

Heather thought for a moment that her eyes were playing tricks on her. But after taking an additional look, as sure as she was standing there, the Santa surely smiled back at her. She stood there in wonder. How could this be? It was a question that would go unanswered today as she hears her father call "Hey, Heather!"

Looking to where her dad is standing, she sees him motioning to her. "Come over here" he says. "I want to take your picture next to this enormous wreath."

Heather looks around the tree to see a huge wreath that looks exactly like the Christmas tree located next to it. The only added feature is the Bronner's logo worked in at the top just under the bow. It is mounted upon a well-crafted wooden bench designed so you could sit in front or stand behind it to have your picture taken.

"Would you like your picture taken in front of it or behind it?" asks Harrison as she makes her way over to him.

"Behind!" she quickly answers, darting behind the wreath before her dad could change her mind. Behind the wreath Heather hops on the ledge that has been built there, situating herself in just the right position to do what has come into her mind. Without hesitation she sticks her head completely through the center of the wreath, cocking it in an unusual angle, plants a great big quirky smile on her face and yells "CHEEZZZ!!!"

Harrison chuckles at her mischievous ways and quickly snaps the picture on his I-Phone.

"That's cute, Sweetie" her mother tells her as she begins to laugh. "I told you Harrison that she'd have fun here today."

"Does that mean you owe mommy another dollar, Daddy?" quips Heather.

"See what you started here" he tells Audrey with a smile. "And to answer your question, young lady, the answer is no. I don't owe Mommy another dollar. Now come on out in front so I can get a couple of pics of you and your mom together."

Heather's first thought is to pop through the center of the wreath and really shock her parents but she figures something would go wrong and she'd get into big trouble. She decides it would be better to jump down from her perch in back of the wreath and come around to the front.

As she comes in front of the wreath, Audrey joins her and they sit down on the bench in front. They snuggle up in a cute and cuddly pose just as Harrison snaps off a couple shots of them. "My two beautiful ladies" he says to them admiring his handiwork. He thinks to himself *"This is going to be a wonderful day"*.

Tucking away his phone, Harrison sees a newspaper stand with the day's current edition of the *Frankenmuth News*. Next to the stand is a large bin full of pamphlets, full of information on the store, shops, and other attractions of the city. He begins to leaf through the bin, picking out pamphlets that catch his interest. Audrey comes to join him while Heather begins to wander around the lobby.

There are so many decorations to see. Looking above the door where they came in, she sees a snow drifted ledge with toy soldiers sitting up them. The other ledges around the area are also snow covered. Some have Christmas trees, while others have angels, snowmen or some other Christmas scene. Each of the ledges have a window just below it that is trimmed with handcrafted shutters that have been painted a magnificent shade of Christmas green and each have a Christmas tree with a star carved out in its center. The ceiling itself is lined with a variety of Christmas lights and multi-colored snow flakes.

As she continues her tour around the lobby she spots a huge alcove to the left of the main doors of the store. It is trimmed out with a lovely, artistically crafted, life-sized Nativity, complete with palm ferns. It is simply amazing to her how they managed to get that into a spot that really doesn't look that big in her eyes. Heather brings her sight back down to a sign that has a big red dot in its center. The sign read…

Bronner's…A World Favorite Meeting Point

As Heather looks over the sign she notices the words MEETING and POINT are more pronounced than the rest of the phrase. Around this phrase she sees there are other words written in foreign languages; German, Italian, and others, a total of over thirty that mean meeting point. She thinks this is pretty cool that people from all over the world would come to visit Bronner's.

All this looking around has made her thirsty. As she is about to say something to her parents, Heather spots drinking fountains next to the sign she has taken an interest in. Even though she is pretty sure they weren't there before, it is neat they happened to be there when she needs them. Moseying over to the fountain that is just her height, Heather presses the button allowing the water to run for a moment before bending in to get her drink.

As she gets her drink she observes a couple of oil paintings above it. One is of Wally Bronner; the other is of his wife, Irene Bronner. She stops to look at the portraits of these two people. Smiling, they look warm, happy, and inviting. Before she can think too much about these people she hears a voice emanating over near the wreath and Christmas tree.

Turning she sees to the right of the entrance, a 32" wide-screen television sitting on top of an oversized present. Heather walks over to investigate. The present is sitting behind a wooden fence draped with pine garland and bows. Surrounding the present are Christmas trees, massive snow drifts made of cotton, and oversized gingerbread men decorations.

As she draws close to the television, she realizes the voice coming from it is the man in the painting above the drinking fountain, Wally Bronner. His gentle voice further piques her interest, and she becomes immediately engrossed in the video that is playing on the screen. As she sits down to watch, she sees, according to the sign sitting on one of the fence posts in front of the present, it is *"The World of Bronner's"*.

2

Heather sits there for a few minutes, listening to Wally Bronner explain the history of his store. The original thought of what she wants to do suddenly crosses her mind again…SANTA.
She wants to see Santa!

"Mom! Dad! C'mon! Let's go see, Santa!" yelling at them as she quickly rushes to her parents, as they are still going over and looking through the pamphlets.

"Okay, Heather" her father tells her. "But we are also here to shop and look around. We have plenty of time to see Santa and we're not in any rush, okay?"

"Okay" she responds in a disappointed tone.

Harrison and Audrey finish picking out the pamphlets they want and begin to head into the store. As they enter, Heather looks up to see a plaque above the door casing with this inscription on it…

20 C + M + B 14

"What does that mean, Dad?" she asks pointing to the plaque.

Giving it a look, Harrison responds "I'm not quite sure, Sweetie, but I'm sure the nice lady at the desk knows" pointing towards the information desk that is just ahead.

Heather ignores the comment for a moment, as she is concentrating on following the snowflakes placed upon the ground that leading one right into the store. As Heather and her parents enter into the store, they find the area open and very spacious. It is decorated around the perimeter with Nativity's of varying looks and sizes. The one set up next to the information desk is close to life-sized and is set under a simplistic manger. It contains the store motto on a ribbon with the Star of Bethlehem in the center. Heather reads…

Enjoy CHRISTmas. It's HIS Birthday.

Enjoy Life. It's HIS Way.

The meaning of this motto Heather understands somewhat, but doesn't realize that it will become clearer later during her visit.

She turns to find a huge, red Christmas ornament hanging off a stand in the center of the area. The area, surrounded by a little white picket fence, has been filled with cotton snow, presents, and garland. Placed on the ornament itself, in a deep white, is the face of Wally Bronner with his name in script beneath it. Though it was pretty cool to her she was unsure of why it was there. Another question she would ask the lady at the desk.

Approaching the counter, Harrison spies a posted sign next to it that reads…

Santa Registration Booth

Located In Section 1

At The South Entrance

Upon reaching the counter, a pleasant grandmotherly lady named Irene greets the family warmly "Welcome to Bronner's. Is there something I can help you with today?"

"Yes" responds Harrison. "It says on your sign here that the registration to see Santa is over in Section 1. Which way is that?"

Picking up a map of the store, Irene explains to Harrison how to get over to Section 1 from where they are right now. She gives him the map and explains it shows where certain things they may be interested in are located throughout the store. "If you have any questions at all feel free to come back here or ask anyone in the store. We'll all be more than happy to help you."

"Thanks" say Harrison.

"I have a question, Ma'am."

"Why yes, dear" Irene responds. "What is it I can answer for you?"

"What is that ornament of Mr. Bronner there for? It looks out of place with the rest of the decorations you have in this spot."

"That, dear" Irene explains, "was a gift to the Bronner family from the staff, after Mr. Bronner passed away. We miss him so around here but we know his spirit is always with us. As for why it is here, he so loved the CHIRST of Christmas, because the Nativity represents this, it was a very appropriate place to put it."

"And what about the plaque above the door?" she asks. It has the initials C, M, B with what looks like plus signs between them and the year."

"You are very inquisitive for a little girl of your age" comments Irene. She explains to Heather "It is a custom in many European countries such as Germany, Austria, and the Czech Republic. The plus signs between them are actually crosses. On Epiphany, which is January 6, this is done to commemorate the wise-men being led by the Star of Bethlehem to the manger. Those Magi were Caspar, Melchior, and Balthasar. Now many interpret the three letters as the initials of those names, however, they actually originate from the Latin phrase of "Christus Mansem Benedicat" which translates into "May Christ bless this home". It is a religious custom that believes the Lord resides with His people throughout the year."

Heather stands there for a moment looking confused when her dad asks her "Did you understand all that?"

"Yes, I did" she answers him, then looks at Irene "Thank you very much, ma'am for the explanation."

"You're very welcome, dear. You have a fun time here today! I'm sure you'll see and learn a lot while you're here."

"Thank you, I will" Heather tells her. "Bye" she says to Irene, waving to her.

"Goodbye, dear" responds Irene returning her wave. As she watches Heather and her family disappear into the mass of people in the store, she knows her statement will come true by days end.

3

Rounding the corner and getting into the heart of the store Heather's parents split apart as Heather walks up between them. "What do you think?" they ask in unison.

Heather is speechless and overwhelmed by the sheer size and scope of what she sees. All kinds of Christmas decorations, trims, and displays stretch as far as the eye can see. Her response to them is simply "WOW!"

They make their way through the crowded store towards the South Entrance, stopping along the way to take a peak at whatever caught Heather's or Audrey's attention. Even Harrison wasn't immune from this, as he did it too even though he continued to tell them "Come on ladies! Plenty of time to look around. Let's get registered for Santa, as I'm sure there is going be a wait.

And a wait he was certainly right-on about. Arriving at the South Entrance, they see a small well-crafted booth. The booth had a very decorative Merry Christmas sign in the center and was decorated with

lighted garland laced with red bows and nutcrackers. Next to the booth
was a sign that read…

Santa Name Tags

And

Registration

Here

As the family approaches the booth they are greeted warmly by a
young lady named Rebekah. "Welcome to Bronner's. Does your child
wish to see Santa today?"

"Yes, she does in a very big way" Harrison responds to her.

Picking up a name tag Rebekah asks "What is your daughter's name?"

"Heather" responds Harrison.

Rebekah writes Heather's name in a very fancy fashion upon the name
tag. She places a small Santa face sticker in the lower right corner of the
tag and motions for Heather to come over to her. Peeling the tag apart
she puts it on the front of Heather's shirt and explains "Now listen for
the jingle bell announcement that calls for children with your Santa
sticker. When you hear that you'll come back just past here to Section 4,
which is right over there" she tells them pointing to where they will need
to be.

"Sounds good. We'll keep our ears open, won't we, Heather"
Harrison tells her as she nods in agreement. "Thank you very much" he
tells Rebekah.

"You're very welcome. Have fun, Heather!"

With a Cheshire grin upon her face, Heather and her dad rejoin her
mom and return to browsing the store.

4

Though Heather is fascinated by all that she sees, her attention is continually focused on the occasional jingle announcements of what group of children Santa was seeing next. Her hopes were dashed many a time hearing snowmen, angels, Christmas tress, everything but Santa stickers.

Then she heard her stomach rumble, and that took her mind off seeing Santa for a moment. "Dad, I'm hungry. Can we get something to eat?"

Audrey concurs with her daughter. "I'm getting a little famished myself. I could use a bite, too."

"Well, if I'm not mistaken, they have a little café here" Harrison tells them, taking a look at the map. "Looks like its just up ahead of where we are right now. So we can swing in for a bite while we wait."

"Sounds good" Audrey says, "What do you think, Heather?"

"Definitely!" she exclaims without any hesitation.

As the family makes there way to the Season's Eatings Snack Area and are about to get in line, they hear the familiar sound of the jingle bells ringing followed by the announcement of…

> *"For boys and girls waiting for Santa, Santa is now ready*
> *to see children that have a Santa sticker on their name tags.*
> *Will those boys and girls with a Santa sticker on their name*
> *tag, please return to Santa's Workshop located in Section 4."*

Heather immediately perks up and gleefully shrieks "THAT'S ME! Let's go, Dad!"

"But I thought you were hungry?" Harrison says to her looking a bit confused.

"I am! But I can wait till after I see Santa! Come on, Dad! Come on! Santa's waiting!!!"

"Alright, already!" replies Harrison. "Guess the snack will just have to wait" stating the obvious as he rolls his eyes at Audrey.

"Think its bad now...wait till she's a teenager" Audrey informs him.

"Don't remind me!" he retorts as they do a 180 turn and head the way they had just come from, back through the store to Santa's Workshop in Section 4.

The

Santa

Swap

"Christmas waves a magic wand over this world and behold, everything is softer and more beautiful."

\- *Norman Vincent Peale*

Chapter 5

1

"C'mon, Mom! C'mon, Dad! Santa's waiting!" pleads Heather as she walks quickly towards Santa's Workshop, getting a good distance ahead of her parents.

"Slow it down, Heather" Audrey tells her.

"Yeah, Heather, slow down. Santa isn't going anywhere. He's got way too many children to see. You'll get to see him, so just relax."

Relax. That is exactly what Harrison is going to do. He knows without a shadow of a doubt that there is going to be a line. Bronner's is extremely busy today. Lots of children to see Santa so there is no rush. Luckily, they are in the middle of the store when the announcement was made. They don't have that far to backtrack. He is very thankful for that. If they had been clear at the other end of the store, he and Audrey might have to sprint just to keep up with their daughter. Walking at a brisk pace through the crowded store is bad enough.

Before they know it they are at Santa's Workshop, just as Harrison thought, there is a line, a very long line. That doesn't seem to bother Heather one bit as she proudly inserts herself in line. For her, she is that much closer to seeing Santa.

Harrison and Audrey, now finally caught up with their daughter, make their way through the line to Heather. The line, to their surprise, is moving at a pretty good pace unlike the ones at the mall.

Audrey notices that kids and parents are being moved into two separate lines. Leaning into Harrison, she quietly whispers to him "They must have two Santas."

Harrison gives the setup a quick once over, then proceeds to tell Audrey without whispering "They'd almost have to have two Santas with so many kids this time of year."

"HARRISON!" Audrey scolds slapping him upside the head. "You'll ruin it for Heather, as well as the other children, if you don't keep it down" she informs him in a more hushed tone.

"Sorry" he tells her.

Composing himself, he looks up ahead to see an employee give him the "not cool" look and motions him to keep quiet. She then mouths to him "*It's a secret. And there is only one!*"

He finds that one a little hard to believe but gives the employee a wink and the okay sign just to play along. That is followed by another smack to the back of the head from Audrey. "Keep it up, mister, and all you'll find under the tree this year is a boxful of switches! Don't spoil it! Why do you think I whispered?!"

"Sorry!" Harrison says somewhat embarrassed by his actions. Audrey is right, and his daughter will tell him that Santa isn't going to put anything in his stocking this year but a lump of coal. Either way, he knows that shutting up is the better part of valor at this point in time.

Less than ten minutes passes. They are next to be placed at the end of two lines. He can tell that Heather is getting excited. The smile on her face keeps growing as she gets closer, and at this point, she is almost there.

Out of the blue, a Bronner employee comes from behind the right curtained line and smiles at Heather. "Hi, Heather!" she says cheerfully. "I'm Lisa. You ready to see Santa?"

"I've waited all *day* to see him!" Heather explains anxiously.

"Well I know for a fact…that he can't wait to see you!" Lisa tells her.

Harrison and Audrey look at each other, both thinking the same thought. This is rather odd. They did not do this with any of the other children. That thought is quickly shattered as Lisa asks the rest of the kids in line the same question. They all respond with a loud and resounding **YES!**

Drawing back the red curtain, Lisa ushers them in. She tells everyone "Santa is waiting just around the corner. Have fun!" though she is looking directly at Heather.

2

Heather and her parents make their way down the makeshift hallway. The walls are designed to look like a log cabin near the bottom, with green-trimmed drywall on the top. Christmas pictures in handcrafted wooden frames line the walls along with brightly, decorated wreaths. In a couple spots along the way are false windows trimmed with wooden shutters similar to those in the lobby area, with SC carved artistically in their centers instead of Christmas trees. The scenes behind the trim appear so realistic that if you didn't look close you would think you are actually looking outside into a winter wonderland.

They round the corner, and the hallway opens up into a study built upon a small, oak platform, triangular in shape. In each corner stand gorgeous Christmas trees, fully decorated and flanked by oversized nutcrackers that are just as tall.

The wall to the left is decorated with a couple of wreaths that have Merry Christmas in the center of each; the wall to the right has a desk with a quill pen, blank papers, and a multitude of letters to Santa on it. To each side of the desk is a set of bookcases filled with all manner of Christmas books, decorations and toys; above the desk, in a uniquely carved, crest-like frame, hangs a brilliant portrait of a Victorian Age Santa.

In the far back corner, just to the left of the desk, rests Santa's chair, intricately carved and painted gold, with red velvet cushions. It is nothing less than magnificent to Heather. Next to the chair is another fine-looking carved table covered with snow fluff. The Holy Family rests in its center, while below it sits Santa's oversized sack.

Heather is astonished by all that she sees. Looking up, she spies a toy train track running around the room. An actual working train, complete with whistle, makes its way around the track that is lined with brilliantly wrapped presents of all shapes and sizes.

There is just one thing missing though...Santa.

Heather turns to her parents, about to cry, and asks "Where's Santa?"

Audrey bends down to console her, but before she can respond, they hear a jolly "Ho, ho, ho!"

Heather whips around to see Santa Claus standing there with his arms wide open. She rushes right to him and gives him a humongous bear hug. "Where were you?" she asked.

"I've been here the entire time" Santa responds quite confidently. "Where have you been, Heather? I've been waiting for you."

"Well, we had to get a name tag, and sign in, then we had to wait to be called, and had to come halfway across the store, then wait in line just to see you" she quickly rambles off.

"Slow down, child" says Santa. "That's a lot to take in. Why don't you sit down with Santa and tell him all about it."

Santa escorts her over to his chair, and as he takes his seat, hoists her onto his lap. "So what would you like for Christmas this year?" asks Santa.

Santa listens intently to Heather's long list as Harrison and Audrey both snap photos of Heather with Santa; the other children try patiently to wait their turns.

"That sounds like quite a lot, young lady" Santa tells Heather when she finishes her list. "Santa will certainly try to fulfill your wish list but I might not be able to do it all. I have lots of other good little boys and girls to take care of as well. Not to mention I need to take time to celebrate what the season is all about."

Confused for a moment by Santa's last statement, Heather knows something isn't quite right. And being the little smarty that she is, responds quickly with "I know. But can I ask you a question?"

"Of course, you can ask Santa a question" he says. "What would you like to know?"

Leaning in close to Santa so the other kids can't hear, she slyly asks him "Are you really Santa Claus?"

The response that comes across his face is the tell tale sign to both Harrison and Audrey what Heather just asked. Before they can move to intercede, Santa motions them that it's okay. With a clear and confident tone he tells her "Yes. I am Santa Claus. Would you like learn more about me, and what Christmas is really about?"

"I would very much like that" she answers solemnly.

"This is as long as it is alright with your parents" he informs her.

Looking over to her folks, she pleads with them "Can I, Mom? Can I, Dad?"

Having heard the conversation, Harrison and Audrey look at each other and with a mutual and unspoken understanding turn to Heather and Santa Claus to give their approval.

"Excellent!" exclaims Santa. "However, we can't have all these children waiting while we talk, now can we?"

"No. That wouldn't be fair" she agrees.

"I knew you would say that" he tells her and with a slight wave of his hand everyone in the room, with the exception of Heather and him, seem to freeze in place as if time had just suddenly stopped. He gives her a wink, and she watches in astonishment as the magic begins to unfold.

3

"Take a look behind me" Santa says to Heather.

Heather does and watches as the wall behind her becomes transparent. She looks through it to see a display of a front window of a house. It is decorated with garland and beautiful poinsettias in a flower box underneath. Two huge ball-shaped ornaments sit on either side. One is a deep, brilliant red with **MERRY CHRISTmas** scripted in white gloss on it; the other is a deep royal blue with **SANTA** neatly printed in white gloss. Snowflakes hang above the display and presents are all around.

Between the two ornaments she sees a Santa similar to the one she saw by the tree in the lobby. This one, however, sits right on the ledge with his legs crossed, leaning on a big, white present wrapped in a gold bow. He looks as if he is in deep thought.

What happens next blows Heather's mind. The Santa stretches as if he had been sitting for much too long. Their eyes lock and smiling, the Santa brings a finger to his lips and motions for her to keep still. She does and watches as the Santa hops down from the ledge to walk across the crowded store toward them.

Heather is amazed by the fact that no one else is seeing this. He moves across the store like a ghost, passing through displays and people who are completely unaware. The display Santa passes through the transparent wall which allows it to revert back to normal. Walking up to Santa, he asks "May I take your place for a bit?"

"That would be wonderful" replies the real Santa as he sets Heather off his lap and stands to allow the display Santa to take his place.

Sitting down, the plastic facade fades away and he become a real human-looking Santa. Shaking himself to limber up, he looks at the real Santa telling him "Take your time, Nicholas. I'll be here till you return."

"Many thanks, my friend" replies Nicholas. Turning toward Heather asks "You ready?"

"Yes" she answers, then pauses a moment to ask "But what about my parents?"

"Ah, yes. I almost forgot. Give them this" he tells her, pulling a Bronner's gift card from his coat pocket. "Tell them it's a gift from Ol' St. Nick and to use it for those special decorations that they have always wanted for your home. They know the ones."

Taking the card from Nicholas, she walks down the platform to get her parents attention. Though they were somewhat frozen in time, they appear to be talking to one another. "Yes, Heather. You ready to get something to eat now that you are all set with Santa?" Audrey asks her.

"No, we have things to talk about yet" she responds, sounding very grownup for a girl of only eight. "But he asked me to give you this" she tells them handing the gift card to her dad. "Santa told me to have you guys use it for those *special* decorations you've always wanted for our home. He said you would know the ones. If it's okay with you, I could stay and talk with him while you do your shopping?"

Audrey looks up at Santa and is stunned that this man knows. How he does she is not sure, but at the same time she is entranced by it. "Thank you, Santa. We appreciate it" she tells him.

"You are most welcome, Audrey" responds Nicholas.

"So is it okay?" Heather asks again.

"Yes, its okay with us, Sweetie" Harrison responds. He then tells Santa "It's very nice of you to take the time to do this...but what about all the other kids?"

"I appreciate your concern, Harrison. But my replacement is here so it is no bother at all" Nicolas responds, pointing to the chair where a display-like Santa sits.

"Okay" says Harrison a bit confused, not able to see what Heather and Nicholas can see. "We'll see you in a little while then. Have a good time" he tells her. "And mind your manners" he adds, before turning with Audrey to walk out of the workshop area and back into the store.

Nicholas smiles as he watches them mesh in with all the other shoppers in the store. Once they have gone from sight, he turns to Heather asking "Ready now?"

"Yes. Now I am!" she answers confidently.

"Then follow me, young one" says Nicholas. "There's a lot to tell, and time is of the essence, as they say."

Nicholas walks over to a door that stands behind his chair. "After you" he tells her, motioning her in.

Unafraid, Heather walks through the door, followed by Nicholas. He gives a quick wink back into the workshop as he closes the door. Upon the door clicking shut, the children and their parents return to life, and all runs as it had before, none being the wiser of what just transpired.

Proper

Introductions

"Christmas is a season for kindling the fire for hospitality in the hall, the genial flame of charity in the heart."

- Washington Irving

Chapter 6

As Nicholas closes the door to the workshop area, a dim light comes on. The room they have entered is small, but cozy, and within a couple of steps, Nicholas is in front of a door at the opposite end.

Grasping the handle, he opens the door. "After you, Heather" and escorts her through.

They emerge in the dining area of the Season's Eatings Snack Area. The dining area is very warm and inviting. Booths line the walls while tables are positioned throughout. All the table tops are a Christmas red, trimmed in a rich wood. The chairs and booths match the wood in the tables and are covered with padding of an evergreen color. The walls of the room are adorned with brightly decorated wreaths, strategically placed. A variety of paintings of the German country sides remind Nicholas of home.

The makeshift windows are reflective and trimmed out with stained wooden shutters containing Christmas tree centers like those in the lobby. The shutters are made from wood of the trees that had been cleared from the Bronner property during one of its expansions. Light fixtures in the ceiling are lined with wreaths and decorated with Coca Cola glass ornaments.

Heather takes it all in when suddenly she realizes the Season's Eatings Snack Area is halfway across the store from where they started. She can't fathom how this is possible considering they only took a few steps from the workshop entrance door to here. It just can't be possible.

What also doesn't seem possible is that there is no one in the store. Not a single soul! Not even her mom and dad. The place is completely deserted, a ghost town. Heather turns to Nicholas to inquire, but is taken aback by his appearance.

No longer in his traditional red, fur lined suit and cap, Nicholas appears to Heather as he was when the Lord had come to give him this task…dressed in a yellow shirt, brown lederhosen, suspenders, wool sox, and black boots. His long flowing green overcoat has shortened a bit, and because he indoors he is sans his velvet Bavarian style hat.

Judging by the look he sees upon her face, explanations are in order. First, perhaps, something to drink and a small snack to help break the ice a bit "Would you like something to drink and a snack to tide you over till dinner later?" asks Nicholas. "Perhaps a hot cocoa and a warm pretzel?" he suggests.

"That sounds really good! Thank you" replies Heather.

Heading to the front of the snack area, Nicholas returns a couple of minutes later with two Bavarian style pretzels, a hot cocoa for Heather and a cup of coffee for himself. Setting them on the table she has chosen, he takes a pretzel and the cocoa and gives it to her. Heather hasn't realized how hungry she actually is since she has been so consumed with seeing Santa.

Breaking a bit of his pretzel off, Nicholas dips it in his coffee and enjoys, as he watches Heather wolf down her pretzel. He can see that she is both puzzled and intrigued, and it's time for him to get to the task at hand.

"I believe proper introductions are in order" Nicholas tells her. "Allow me to introduce myself, my name is Nicholas" he says extending his hand to her.

Though only eight, she is aware of the social courtesy of one extending one's hand to you. Extending hers to shake his, she replies "It's nice to meet you, Mr. Nicholas. My name is Heather Fahs."

"I appreciate the courtesy, Heather, but you don't have to address me as mister. Just Nicholas will do."

Heather nods her head in acknowledgment quickly asking "So is it as cold at the North Pole this time of year as it is here in Michigan?" She takes a big sip of the hot cocoa he brought her.

"*Very clever*" he thinks to himself. Being just as clever, he responds "I'm sure it probably is, though I wouldn't know, as I don't live at the North Pole." He then takes a sip of his coffee.

Heather is shocked at the response. "But if you are Santa Claus, Mr. Nicholas" keeping the courtesy she was raised with (which is a rarity these days), "Then why don't you live at the North Pole? And if you don't live at the North Pole, then where *do* you live?"

"You are a very intelligent young lady, Heather. You are going to find, over the course of our visit, many things that have been attributed to me over the years just aren't so. As far as where I really live, I live in a cabin in a beautiful wooded area in the Bavarian Forest, just outside a little village named Zell, in Germany."

Heather is blown away by his answer. She begins to doubt that Mr. Nicholas is actually Santa. The only thing that keeps a shred of this alive is the other events, which she can't explain, that have happened throughout the day.

Finishing her cocoa, after several minutes of silence, she asks "Are you really, Santa Claus? Do you really exist? Some of my friends say you don't and my parents, well let's just say they do a good job keeping the truth a mystery."

Nicholas looks at her and sees confusion. He is aware, by the gifts the Lord has given him that she is very intelligent and with his guidance she will see the truth of it all. "Walk with me" he tells her as they get up from their seats, depositing the trash in the bins.

Nicholas leads her back towards the Santa Workshop Area, and with no one in the store, the way back is much easier. Within a couple of minutes they approach Section 6 of the store. Here are abundant displays of *Department 56* items (*Department 56* is known for buildings and villages for collectors to create scenes for decorating throughout the year).

One area of the *Department 56* section contains a variety of historic American monuments. One portion depicts New York City. As Heather comes in front of it, she is immediately drawn in. Why she is not sure.

Once she is completely captivated by the display, Nicolas responds to her earlier inquiry. He says "To answer your earlier question, Heather...yes, I really am Santa Claus. I really do exist though just not the way you've grown up knowing. I know you are somewhat confused by this, and you harbor doubts. You are not unlike other children your age I have had the pleasure of knowing. Your skepticism is very reminiscent of another girl I once knew.

"Who was she?" asks Heather taking her attention off the display to look up at him.

"A young lady of eight, much like yourself, whose name is Virginia O'Hanlon."

Yes, Virginia

There Is A

Santa Claus

"*Yes, Virginia, there is a Santa Claus. He exists as certainly as love and generosity and devotion exist, and you know that they abound and give to your life its highest beauty and joy.*"

- *Francis Pharcellus Church*
From the Editorial Page
Of the New York Sun
September 21, 1897

Chapter 7

1

Virginia O'Hanlon. The sound of Nicholas saying her name seems to focus Heather's attention even more toward the display of New York City buildings that lie before her. With her focus engaged on that which lies before her, Heather fails to notice that her surroundings are in a state of flux.

The Christmas surroundings of Bronner's begin to melt away like an icicle exposed to a warm beam of sunlight, into a bright, comfortable, sunny autumn afternoon in New York City. Hearing the chirping of birds in a nearby tree snaps Heather out of her trance-like state, she abruptly discovers she's no longer at Bronner's. She is no longer staring down at a display but actually staring at a real house, one quite unlike she has ever seen.

This house looks like something out of a movie she has seen her parents watch, no *grandparent*. It's very simplistic, red bricked with a peaked roof. One might say it was Victorian, maybe Queen Ann, in design but would be thrown by the unique and intricate touches of irregular quoining around the window openings.

Somewhat alarmed by what she sees, Heather swiftly looks to make sure that Nicholas is still there. He looks down at her with grace and a comforting smile that sets her immediately at ease. "It's quite alright" he assures her. "You haven't gone mad."

"Where are we, Mr. Nicholas?" she asks a bit perplexed.

"West 95th Street, New York City, in the year 1897" Nicholas informs her. "As a matter of fact, #115 here in front of us just happens to be the home of the young lady I was just speaking about."

"1897?" questions Heather. "But, Mr. Nicholas, its 2014. How can we be back in the past? That isn't possible."

"It is possible. I'll explain a bit later. Right now there is someone you need to meet" pointing to a little girl coming down the sidewalk toward the house. She is very pretty with dark, shoulder length hair, dressed in a very simple, yet elegant white dress. She is picture perfect, with the exception of her eyes which are very red and puffy, as though she has been crying recently.

"HELLO!" Heather yells to her.

The little girl doesn't respond just simply rushes up the steps straight into the house.

"That was rude!" Heather says to Nicholas with a disgusted, protruded look on her face. "The least she could've done was to say "Hi"!"

Nicholas touches her shoulders to calm her. "The fault is not hers, Heather. The fault would be mine. You see, though we are actually here in the past, we cannot be seen nor heard. Try to think of it like Charles Dickens's story of *"A Christmas Carol"* where the ghosts are showing Scrooge events of his past, present, and future. The same applies to us" explains Nicholas.

"I love that story" Heather says, "So I know what you are talking about."

"Very good" responds Nicholas. "Shall we go in to hear what young Virginia is telling her papa?"

"But we haven't been invited in. It wouldn't be right."

"You have a very true heart, Heather. Don't ever lose that. In this instance, I assure you, I have permission, and it'll be okay" he convinces her with a gleam in his eye.

Heather takes his extended hand and instantaneously they are inside the study of Dr. Philip F. O'Hanlon, police surgeon and Deputy Coroner for the city. Sitting in his chair, he quietly reads the daily edition of *"The New York Sun"*. They stand silently and watch as history unfolds before their eyes.

2

"Papa!" announces Virginia as she walks into the room with a quiver in her voice.

"Yes, Virginia" he says looking up from his paper to see that his daughter has been crying. "What is wrong?"

"It's my friends. They were picking on and making fun of me today."

"Why would they do such a thing, Virginia?"

"Because, I told them that Santa Claus was real. They told me that Santa Claus doesn't exist at all. That he's nothing but a fake!"

"I see" her papa responds.

"Papa…does Santa Claus exist?"

The question throws Dr. O'Hanlon. For one so young how do you respond to such a question? You want to be truthful to your child and not lie. However, a subject such as this is very tricky at this age, and you don't want to shatter young hopes and dreams. *"How to answer?"* he thought. He didn't want to directly answer the question, so he thought it best to "pass the buck". In a very rational tone he tells her "I would suggest to you, that you write *"The Sun"*, Virginia. Ask them your question. And if you see it in *"The Sun"*, then it is so."

Hearing this many times from her Papa she immediately brightens up and becomes very chipper. Giving her papa a big hug, she states emphatically "Thank you, Papa! I'm going to write *"The Sun"* and find out the real truth!"

"By all means go ahead, Virginia. I'm sure *"The Sun"* will give you the correct answer as it always does."

3

Virginia proceeds directly to her room from her papa's study. Going over to her desk, she pulls out a sheet of paper and a pen and sits down to ponder what to write to the paper. While she is in deep thought, Nicholas and Heather materialize behind her. Heather gazes over Virginia's shoulder with anticipation as to what she is going to say when she puts pen to paper.

Virginia positions herself to write. As she does, Nicholas informs Heather "You are about to witness the writing of one of the most famous letters ever written in history. One that will be remembered for all eternity and will ask the most basic of questions that we have *all* asked at one point in our lives."

They watch as she begins to write...

"Dear Editor,

*I am 8 years old. Some of my little friends say there
is no Santa Claus. Papa says, "If you see it in The Sun,
it's so." Please tell me the truth, is there a Santa Claus?*

Virginia O'Hanlon
115 West Ninety-Fifth Street"

The letter Virginia writes doesn't take her very long. It is simplistic and to the point. Satisfied with what she has written, Virginia folds it up, places it into an envelope, addresses it, and runs downstairs to give it to her papa to mail.

4

"Do you recognize this building, Heather?" Nicholas asks as they appear out of the blue in the streets of New York City.

Getting her bearings, she gives it a once over and responds "Yes. It looks just like the one in the display back at Bronner's…only bigger."

Nicholas chuckles with a familiar laugh. "That it is" he tells her, then explains "This is The Sun Building where Miss O'Hanlon sent her letter. Once it was received, it was given to an editorial writer here by the name of Francis Pharcelus Church. His 500 word reply, which coincidentally will be printed in today's paper precisely on page 6, is destined to become one of the most famous editorials of all time. In fact, it continues to be printed and used from time to time to this day. Would you like to read it?"

"Yes, I would like to very much."

"Very well" Nicholas says. Seeing a newsboy on the corner, Nicholas flags him down. Reaching into his pocket he pulls out a coin, a denomination much larger than needed exchanging it for the paper. "Keep the change for yourself, lad!" he tells the newsboy.

"Thanks, Mister!" he exclaims seeing just how big of a tip he received.

Heather gives Nicholas a strange look, "I thought you said that we couldn't be seen or heard?"

"Indeed, I did. However, it's one of the benefits of being me" he explains as he opens the paper up to page 6 and hands it to Heather. "Here was his response."

Adjusting the paper, Heather reads…

> "**V**irginia, your little friends are wrong. They have been affected by the skepticism of a skeptical age. They do not believe except [what] they see. They think that nothing can be which is not comprehensible by their little minds. All minds, Virginia, whether they be men's or children's, are little. In this great universe of ours man is a mere insect, an ant, in his intellect, as compared with the boundless world about him, as measured by the intelligence capable of grasping the whole of the truth and knowledge.
>
> Yes, Virginia, there is a Santa Claus. He exists as certainly as love and generosity and devotion exist, and you know that they abound and give to your life its highest beauty and joy. Alas! How dreary would be the world if there were no Santa Claus. It would be as dreary as if there were no Virginias. There would be no childlike faith then, no poetry, no romance to make tolerable this existence. We should have no enjoyment except in sense and sight. The eternal light with which childhood fills the world would be extinguished.
>
> Not believe in Santa Claus! You might as well not believe in fairies! You might get your papa to hire men to watch in all the chimneys on Christmas Eve to catch Santa Claus, but even if they did not see Santa Claus coming down, what would that prove? Nobody sees Santa Claus, but that is no sign that there is no Santa Claus. The most real things in the world are those that neither children nor men can see. Did you ever see fairies

*dancing on the lawn? Of course not, but that's
no proof that they are not there. Nobody can conceive
or imagine all the wonders there are unseen and
unseeable in the world.*

*You tear apart the baby's rattle and see what makes
the noise inside, but there is a veil covering the unseen
world which not the strongest man, nor even the united
strength of all the strongest men that ever lived could tear
apart. Only faith, fancy, poetry, love, romance, can push
aside that curtain and view and picture that supernal beauty
and glory beyond. Is it all real? Ah, Virginia, in all this
world there is nothing else real and abiding.*

*No Santa Claus! Thank God he lives, and he lives
forever. A thousand years from now, Virginia, nay,
ten times ten thousand years from now, he will continue
to make glad the heart of childhood."*

Christmas

&

Wally

"You want to know the truth? The truth is no decorations are needed at all at Christmas. What's really needed at Christmas is that we decorate our hearts."

- *Wally Bronner*

Chapter 8

Heather stands stunned at the response Mr. Church has given Virginia. It sure isn't the response she had been expecting to read on such a question. She guesses that he would have answered the question in a very simple and straight forward. Something to the effect of *"Yes, there is a Santa, and he lives at the North Pole;"* not unlike the answers *she* always gets when asking difficult questions that someone doesn't want to take the time to explain. After all, both she and Virginia are only eight.

Being eight isn't an issue in this circumstance Heather thought. Mr. Church really seems to have taken Virginia's question to heart. Instead of giving that *"simple"* answer to the question Virginia has posed to him, Mr. Church's response to her is a much more elaborate, detailed, and in depth one. Smiling, Heather supposes Virginia must feel a tad more grown up after reading this response, similar to how she herself fells right at this moment.

"What a response Virginia got from…" Heather starts to say to Nicholas, stopping in mid-sentence as she looks up from the newspaper editorial. She stands there completely and utterly gobsmacked. No longer is she standing in the streets of New York City, circa 1897, but right in front of the *Department 56* display at Bronner's.

Seeing Heather is more than just a bit confused with the state of affairs, he asks in a very calm, reassuring tone "Remember what I said to you earlier, when we first arrived at number 115 95ᵗʰ Street?"

Thinking back to that moment, Heather responds "You…told me that…I hadn't gone mad."

"That I did. And I promise you now, as I did then, you haven't"

"Then we were really there…in New York City, right? I'm not just imagining things?"

"No, you are not imaging things. Not one bit. We were really there."

"How is that possible?"

"Because I'm Santa Claus" Nicholas states very confidently. "It is one of the many gifts that have been bestowed upon me."

"I know you say that you are Santa Claus, but that wasn't my question" Heather states emphatically. "I asked *how* do you do it?"

"You are very observant," compliments Nicholas, knowing full well he didn't directly answer her question. He is truly beginning to see why the Lord has chosen this girl. Thinking for a moment, Nicholas says to Heather, "In this day, I believe that you would call it time traveling. However, a much better way to explain would be to refer you back to Dickens's "*A Christmas Carol*" story."

"In what way?" she asks.

"Think of my gifts to show you things of the past similar to that of the ghosts within the story. It is a *Divine* gift, and here at Bronner's, very easy to do because it is such magical place. So…still not convinced I'm not Santa Claus?"

"I still have my doubts, but you do make a very good case" Heather responds optimistically.

"I would say progress is being made" Nicholas concurs.

"I do have a question about something that you said, Mr. Nicholas" says Heather.

"What would that be?" asks Nicholas.

"You said that for you to use your gifts here at Bronner's is easy to do because it's a magical place. What makes it such a magical place? Cause to me it's just a store that sells Christmas stuff" retorts Heather.

"Bronner's is much more than just a store that sells Christmas stuff" states Nicholas. "Nevertheless, before I can effectively answer your question as to why Bronner's is such a magical place, I need you to answer a question for me.

"Okay" agrees Heather. "What is it?"

"What is Christmas to you?"

Heather stands silent for a moment before answering "I don't understand what you are asking, Mr. Nicholas."

To clarify, Nicholas explains "What I'm asking is what does Christmas mean to you? Why do you and your family celebrate it, and what meaning does it have for you?"

Heather ponders the question as she unintentionally begins to wander back toward the snack area, looking at all the decorations and trinkets as she walks. Following her with great patience, Nicholas is suddenly flabbergasted and amused as Heather begins to babble a multitude of ideas.

"It's about family, though I don't get along with some of my cousins, going shopping for gifts for others, coming to the mall to see Santa and ask him for lots of presents so I can wake up Christmas morning to open them." She pauses, then quickly adds "and decorating the house up nice and purdy!"

Her response doesn't surprise Nicholas. Most children her age answer in similar fashion; even some adults, sorry to say. "Anything else?" he asks.

"I know I'm missing something, but I can't think of what it is" she states before interrupting Nicholas by blurting "And it is to celebrate the birth of Jesus!"

Smiling, Nicholas sees that she has at least been exposed to the latter though it is not her primary focus. Perhaps it's because her parents didn't make it a focus or it could just simply be the perception of someone her age. Either way, things are so much different today than they were in his time. The belief system throughout the years has become so narrow minded. No matter. He was sent with a task and Nicholas knows Heather was chosen by the Lord for a reason. He knows not to question it, simply accept it.

"Those are all very good answers, Heather. Most children answer as you have. But Christmas is so much more. Yes, it is about family, even those cousins you don't get along with" he tells her with a hint of a grin. "It is also about giving to others you are very right on that account. However, it really isn't about the decorating, though that has become tradition. Though I am part of the season, it is unfortunate that it has become highly commercialized over the years, which I consider to be blasphemous. Now with regards to presents, it is not about the presents that you would like to see under the tree, but undeniably the one greatest gift that was given to us all. That present was Jesus, and Christmas is the day we celebrate his birth."

Heather stands there blown away by Nicholas's answer. She has been told of this by her grandparents and parents. Her family isn't very religious, and it really wasn't a focal point, even though they did put up a

Nativity on the coffee table centered in the living room each year. This connection escapes her.

"Then how could you be Santa if your role has been com-mer-cial-ized? Commercialized. And why shop for decorations in a place like Bronner's if the focus is on the birth of Jesus?" Heather asks a bit confused.

"You are very clever, Heather" Nicholas compliments. "Very intelligent for someone of eight. I give you great credit for that. With regards to me being Santa, and how I come "into the picture," as you say these days, I will get to that in due time yet during our visit. Now as to your other query..."

"What is a query, Mr. Nicholas?" interrupts Heather, then immediately apologizes for her interruption.

"A query is another term for a question. Now as to your query, I mean question, shopping for decorations. We shop for the decorations as a way to help celebrate the season. It has become a tradition to decorate with certain items, as they have a special meaning and relate in some way to the birth of Christ. Decorations such as Christmas Trees and Nativities, to name a few, are used to celebrate the season. Your parents placing your Nativity in the center of the room shows that they know, even at a subconscious level, that Jesus is center of the season and is the reason we celebrate it. Besides of all the places to shop for decorations, Bronner's is simply the best. Not just for the selection, but for one simple fact; they embody the Spirit of Christmas in each and everything single thing they do, everyday. That is something, seriously is lacking in the world of today."

Heather thinks about what Nicholas has just imparted to her. Precipitously, she comes to a halt when she hears the voice of Wally

Bronner emanating from behind her. She listens carefully to what Wally
tells her…

> *"You want to know the truth? The truth is no decorations*
> *are needed at all at Christmas. What is really needed at*
> *Christmas is that we decorate our hearts."*

Turning around, she finds there is no one there. It is still just her and
Nicholas. Then Heather spies the source of the voice. A small television
set, playing a DVD entitled "BCW", rests behind a glass display case.
Investigating further Heather hits upon that she has stopped in front of a
small, humble, but richly appointed alcove that has been dedicated to
Wally Bronner, the originator of Bronner's CHRISTmas Wonderland.

Slowly walking into the alcove, she looks up to see a ribbon banner
that reads…

JOYful Memories   Bronner's Originator

In its center an ornament with the smiling picture of Wally Bronner that
seems to invite her in to learn more. Taking in all that is displayed behind
the glass, she begins moving from one end of the alcove to the other,
studying all the items. Framed newspaper articles on Mr. Bronner;
photographic history of both the family and major events of the store;
awards for various business and philanthropic achievements; specialty
items made personally for Mr. Bronner; and many of Mr. Bronner's
personal effects: his Bavarian hat, trademark red coat, and one of his
many colorful Christmas ties that he wore when he was in the store lined
the alcove.

"Is this the gentleman who created all this?" asks Heather.

"Indeed it is" Nicholas responds with a smile. It is no coincidence
that she has wandered back to this point. This is something that he wants
Heather to see.

Unaware of the importance of this Heather says "Mr. Nicholas, will you please tell me more about him?"

"It would be an honor to do so" responds Nicholas.

2

Nicholas gestures for Heather to take a seat at a small grouping of chairs that are situated in the center of the alcove. Acknowledging the gesture, she takes a seat in one closest to her. As she settles, Nicholas can tell by the look that radiates from her face that he has her undivided attention.

"Wally..." Nicholas starts to say before stopping. "I mean Mr. Bronner" he corrects, remembering Heather's etiquette, "started from very humble beginnings. As a young lad, he began honing his customer service skills working for his Aunt Hattie at Hubinger's Grocery Store." Nicholas produces a picture of a very young Wally Bronner, circa 1941, at his aunt's grocery store.

She looks at the old photo commenting "He was a very handsome young man."

"Indeed he was" states Nicholas continuing his story "In 1943 Mr. Bronner started his first business, sign painting out of his parent's basement, everyday after school. Mr. Bronner was ahead of his time when it came to this trend, considering the number of big name companies that also started from such humble beginnings. But I digress. After graduating from high school in 1945, Mr. Bronner opened his first official shop. There he perfected not only his craft, but his business skills as well. Then in 1951, after meeting some merchants from the city of Clare, who were looking for Christmas decorations for their cities lampposts, he created a line of custom Christmas panels. This marked the start in his very successful career in Christmas decorations. It was also the year he met and married his beautiful wife and soul-mate, Irene. Three years later, in 1954, Mr. & Mrs. Bronner constructed their first permanent store in the heart of Frankenmuth, over half of which was dedicated to Christmas decorations."

Nicholas stops for a moment to point out the pictures within the display cases that coincide with the history he is imparting to her. He allows her to take it in for a moment then continues "Over the next 20 years, Mr. Bronner would expand his business by adding two other buildings. The first he added in 1966, which was called the Tannenbaum Shop; then in 1971 he added the old grocery store where he worked as a teen, renaming it The Bavarian Corner. With the business continuing to grow, it became apparent it was time to consolidate the three of them under one roof. So, in 1976, construction commenced on what would come to be known as "The World's Largest Christmas Store". In 1977 it opened up right where we are today. It has gone through a couple of expansions since then. The rest, as they say, is history."

"Wow!" exclaims Heather as she finishes looking at the photos that illustrate the remainder of his story.

"That is one way to put it, I guess" agrees Nicholas. "Except that isn't the half of it. Yes, Mr. Bronner took his passion, as it was never a job to him, and grew from humble beginnings into the beautiful store you see here today. That, in and of itself, is a great achievement, though an even greater achievement is who Mr. Bronner built his business around. *That* is what makes this place so special.

"Who was that person, Mr. Nicholas?" Heather asks curiously.

"That person Heather was Jesus Christ. In the bible, specifically John 3:16, it says "For God so loved the world, that he gave his only son". Mr.

Bronner's gift, beyond business, was to encourage others to know Jesus, as it was He who gave Mr. Bronner's life true meaning, purpose and was the driving force in everything that he did. Even when he knew the end was near, he never wavered."

Nicholas pulls a small piece of paper from his jacket pocket. Unfolding it carefully he tells Heather "This is a copy of a note that Mr. Bronner wrote to his staff on Good Friday of 2008. Read it and you will see what I'm telling you is true."

Heather takes the note and begins to read it, hearing the voice of Mr. Bronner read it as if he is actually there writing it. He says…

> *"Today's Good Friday was especially GOOD FRIDAY*
> *when our dear family and prayer agreed to the reality that*
> *our loving Lord and Savior – the CHRIST of CHRISTmas –*
> *is ready to receive me into his heavenly kingdom where all*
> *believers in the Creator God will be with him FOREVER*
> *AND EVER…NOTHING COULD BE GREATER!"*

Tears begin to stream like rivers down Heather's cheeks, being moved by such a note. Her hand shakes as she gives it back to Nicholas sobbing the words "Wha…wha…what hap…hap… happened to him?"

"All good things must come to an end, and a great man, Mr. Wally Bronner went to be with his CHRIST of CHRISTmas a couple of days later. It was such a wonderful life." Giving her a hug to console her, Nicholas turns what looks like a negative into a positive by telling her "Don't cry, Heather. Yes, it is sad that he left us, but for Mr. Bronner it was the greatest gift to be called home! He would want nothing more for all of us when our time comes. Open your heart and you can feel the Spirit of Christmas all around you here. It is *this* that makes this such a magical place. Let it in and it will always be with you!"

"I wish I could have met him" she tells Nicholas as she wipes her tears on her sleeve. "He sounds like he was an extraordinary man."

"Indeed he was, and still is, Heather" stopping in mid sentence as he hears the sounds of jingle bells off in the distance, growing louder as the draw nearer to them. Knowing who is coming, he gives Heather a big smile. "Perk up!" he tells her. "There is someone else I would like you to meet" pointing toward a familiar figure coming from the direction of the Season's Eatings Snack Area.

A Tale Of
Two
St. Nicks

"Christmas is the day that holds all time together."

- Alexander Smith

Chapter 9

Heather dries her eyes with a tissue that Nicholas pulled from a pocket inside his jacket. Composing herself, she notices the man approaching them bears a striking resemblance to Mr. Nicholas. In fact, they look like identical twins, and the only real way to tell them apart is by how they are dressed: one in casual attire, the other as a bishop from a church.

"Nicholas, my friend!" he exclaims giving Nicholas a great embrace "So good to see you!"

"Good to see you as well, St. Nicholas. It has been awhile."

"That it has, old friend. And who is this lovely young miss you have with you?!"

"This, St. Nicholas, is Heather Fahs."

St. Nicholas extends his hand. As she returns the gesture, he shakes her hand and he tells her warmly "It is a pleasure to meet you, Heather. I am St. Nicholas."

"It's very nice to meet you as well" she says to him. "But I'm a bit confused. You say you are St. Nicholas" she says pointing to him. Then points to Nicholas and says "He is Mr. Nicholas and claims to also be Santa Claus. And St. Nicholas is also another name for Santa Claus. So are the two of you related or something?"

The two Nicholases look at each other and without a word between them know what the other is thinking. After a moment of silence, Nicholas tells Heather "We are one and the same."

His answer really blows Heather's little mind, confusing her even further. Looking at both of them, she ponders for a moment, and then speaks. Pointing to St. Nicholas "So you are St. Nicholas, a bishop."

"Yes" St. Nicholas responds.

Then turning and pointing at Nicholas "You are Mr. Nicholas, also Santa Claus."

"Correct" Nicholas responds.

"And you are telling me, you are both the same person?" Heather inquires.

"YES" they respond in perfect unison.

Heather shakes her head in an attempt to clear the cobwebs of confusion from her brain.

Before she can say another word, St. Nicholas states "I am about ready to do a little program here that I think will clear things up a bit for you, Heather. It will also help Nicholas prove he is truly Santa Claus in a practical way that I believe you will be more than able to understand. Would you care to come see it?"

"Sure" Heather replies.

"Then it is settled. Meet me in Bronner's Program Center in Section 2 shortly, and I'll get started." Making his leave, he pauses for a moment, turns to Nicholas to say "By the way, it would be very nice to have an audience for this," motioning to the lack of people in Bronner's. "Works better that way, don't ya know."

Understanding what St. Nicholas means, "Of course. How silly of me" and with a snap of his fingers St. Nicholas is replaced by the hustling and bustling of all the shoppers that have come to visit this day.

"Where'd he go?!" asks Heather looking around frantically to see where he went.

"To make preparations for the program he is giving. Follow me and you'll see soon enough" Nicholas assures her.

"Okay" she says taking his hand as they head to the store's program center in Section 2.

Saint

To

Santa

"Christmas is a bridge. We need bridges as the river of time flows past. Today's Christmas should mean crafting happy hours for tomorrow and reliving those of yesterday."

- Gladys Taber

Chapter 10

1

Nicholas escorts Heather into the program center. At the front of the modest-sized room sits a small stage draped with a red velvet curtain around its edge. Red velvet curtains also drape the back of the stage making it look like a small movie screen. The bottoms of the curtains are lined with bright poinsettia plants. On each of the stage's back corners are large scale versions of the Holy Family, each a little different from the other. On each of the front corners rests, a set of identical angels, playing instruments. Set in a crescent shape in front of the stage are three distinct sections of chairs, five rows within each section.

This may be what is intended of this room, but it's what lies around the room that leaves even a little girl of eight breathless. Heather first notices around the back of the room is a large display case filled with one of the largest collections of Hummel figurines around. They are simplistic in the beauty they portray.

Along the adjacent wall is another display case with a good sized collection of Precious Moments and Snow Babies figurines. According to the signage above them on the outside of the case, they have either been retired or have been suspended from production.

As she continues to scan the room, she sees an old organ with displays of early paintings done by Wally Bronner and old 60's style décor of oversized bells and ornaments from outdoor displays hanging from the ceiling. A display case houses official White House ornaments. Hanging on a wall adjacent to it, a four pane case, resembling a set of cathedral windows. It houses a wide variety of very old glass ornaments from the Lauscha/Bohemia region. These ornaments date back as far as 1847.

All of these items are impressive to be sure, but pale in comparison to the real focus of the room. Although it is the store's program center, it is also home to the store's vast Nativity collection, which is the heart of the Christmas season.

Oversized outdoor Nativities adorn the upper perimeter of the room while smaller more traditional ones line shelves of multiple display cases. Each one is unique, and they represent all corners of the world.

Fascinated by all that she sees, Heather's focus is broken by a young Bronner's employee who enters the room. Making her way to the front of the stage, she looks around the room briefly, then motions for quiet.

Nicholas sees this and turns to Heather "We should take our seats." He users her to one on the end in the center of the front row. The rest of the audience sees this and follows lead.

As the audience starts to settle, the young employee introduces herself. "Good afternoon, everyone" she begins. "My name is Julie, and I want to thank you all for coming today. Saint Nicholas will be here in a few moments. So if we wait quietly, we'll be able to hear his bells. And the first person who hears his bells, raise your hand. Now listen" she tells them, bringing a finger to her lips.

The room becomes very quiet and still as Julie makes her way toward the program center's entrance. She stands at the doorway for a couple of minutes then makes a nod as if getting a signal from another employee outside the room. Turning, Julie returns to the front of the stage and stands, looking out towards the eager audience.

At that moment, the jingling of bells can be heard in the distance, outside the program center. As they grow louder, a child in the audience exclaims gleefully, "Here he comes!"

Seeing the person ringing the bells as he crosses the threshold of the door, Julie proudly announces "Boys and girls, ladies and gentlemen, Saint Nicholas!"

The audience claps and children of all ages watch in awe as Saint Nicholas, the Bishop of Myra, makes his entrance into the room. Going to the front of the stage, Saint Nicholas places a large green sack he carries with him down in the front corner. Her turns to Julie and accepts a microphone she hands to him. With a nod of thanks, Saint Nicholas turns to address the excited audience.

2

"Well hello, everyone!" he greets them in a deep, jolly voice. "Are you all in the Christmas Spirit?" he asks, holding the microphone out to the audience for a response.

The reaction is weak at best.

"I can't hear you!" he says.

The response this time is much more enthusiastic as he explains "This is the day the Lord has made let us rejoice, and be glad. You know this time of year is a time of preparation. What are *you* doing to get ready for Christmas?" He pauses for a moment, and with no answer from the audience, asks the question again with a slight difference. "What are you doing in your *home* to get ready for Christmas?"

Saint Nicholas looks around the room and catches a glimpse of a young boy who raises his hand. He goes over, extending the microphone to the young lad, who responds "Shopping."

"Shopping for gifts for other people" responds Saint Nicholas. "Okay, what else?" he asks, seeing another child raise her hand. Moving over to this young girl and extending the microphone to her, she responds "Decorating."

Nodding his head in agreement, he tells the audience "Decorating the home, and tree, and things, yeah. Anything else?" he asks, looking for a much more specific answer that is not being given.

Scanning the room one more time, he spies another small child. Going over to him, his response is the same as the previous child's though his answer isn't picked up by the microphone for the audience to hear. Taking a step back, Saint Nicholas tells everyone "He is just to decorate in general. You're not particular he's just gonna plain decorate." He gives a hearty, jolly "Ho, ho, ho" and returns to the front of the stage.

"Well, I'll tell you how to get ready for Christmas in a different way" he explains. He continues "First of all, I'll tell you where I came from and how you came to know me as Santa Claus; and secondly, I'm going to let you in on a *well kept secret* in the culture…why I'm so jolly at Christmas time. First of all, do you know where I was born? Can anybody guess?"

"At the North Pole!" someone immediately shouts.

"At the North Pole" Saint Nicholas repeats adding quickly "No, you're getting cold" to which the audience chuckles.

"BETHLEHEM!" a young girl blurts, with a little help and encouragement from her mother.

"Bethlehem, well now your getting warmer" he tells her. "I was born not far from Bethlehem in the Mediterranean, a place called Patara. That was in Asia Minor that's modern day Turkey" he chuckles. "If you think

about it, here I'm in all these Thanksgiving parades and now they call my
place of origin, Turkey."

This notion causes the audience to laugh as well as Saint Nicholas.
Standing tall and proud he continues his story. "My mother and father
were devout Christians and loved Jesus very much. And I had thought at
an early age about following into the ministry, following Jesus. But then a
sad thing happened. You know my mother and father where very wealthy
merchants. My father sold textiles, that's cloth, to make clothing in my
day. And there was an epidemic, a sickness, went through our little town
of Patara. And my mother and father were Christians they had to help
the sick and the dying. I'm sad to say, they both got sick too, and died
helping the sick. Being their only child boys and girls, Saint Nicholas
here, I inherited their fortune."

He pauses for a moment, looking sad that this has happened to him.
He tells the audience in a moment of reflection "But I remembered an
incident, a story, something that happened during the time of Jesus. It's
recorded in the New Testament."

This suddenly perks Saint Nicholas up and he explains "One day, a
rich young man came up to Jesus and said "I want to be one of your
followers." And Jesus said "Sell what you have. Give to the poor. One
day you'll have treasure in Heaven. Then come and follow me." Did the
rich young man follow Jesus? No. He went away sad. I thought to
myself, wait a minute, now I'm a rich young man too. And bearing my
mom and dad's fortune, I saw sickness and suffering all around me. And I
wanted to follow Jesus in the ministry, so I decided to sell everything I
had to help the sick, the poor, and the dying. In fact, I heard about a *man*,
who had three grown daughters and boys and girls, he was so poor he
could barely feed his daughters or provide a roof over their heads, they

were about to lose their home. Well, Saint Nicholas here got drift of that and so I got together three bags of gold coins."

Saint Nicholas pauses slightly, and pretends to hold something in his hand. Creeping across the stage he explains "And I crept up in the middle of the night and threw those three bags of gold coins in the window. That was the first of my midnight visits. That's the reason, to this very day I always deliver gifts under the cover of night. You know Jesus said "When you do acts of charity...don't let one hand know what the other one's up to.""

Laughter erupts from the audience at this statement partially from the way Saint Nicholas delivers it. To others it's humorous due to the ring of truth it has to it. This moment of laughter gives Saint Nicholas a chance to catch his breath. Collecting his thoughts, he proceeds with the presentation.

"Boys and girls" he says giving a long pause "I'm one of the first saints around not because I died a heroic death, but because I loved Jesus. You know these saints like Paul and Peter they had to die a martyr's death, huh. Martyr's death? And I thought to myself, wait a minute; there are other ways to be holy besides dying. I was thrown in prison for seven years under a terrible Pagan persecution, then I was released. Then I thought to myself, wait a minute, how about living the virtues of faith, hope, and love to a *bigger* degree. And so I was known as the friend of poor families, and children of course, especially, huh.

Now in the middle ages, some religious sisters in France decided to honor me on the eve of my feast day in December. Does anyone know when Saint Nicholas Day is? December..." he begins in an attempt to lead the audience towards the answer.

"SIXTH" a young, confident gentleman yells from the back of the program center.

"Sixth" Saint Nicholas concurs continuing "And on the eve of my feast, that's December five, some sisters took up a collection for the needy and poor. Clothing and toys for poor boys and girls, and guess who they had deliver them? Saint Nicholas! Pretty soon that tradition spread like wildfire throughout Europe, and pretty soon I was delivering things to gift them unto the poor, but to all the good boys and girls everywhere.

Boys and girls in Holland today, do you realize I don't arrive on Christmas Eve, I still arrive on the eve of my feast. Saint Nicholas Eve, December five, they call it Sinterklaas Eve. Sinterklaas means Saint Nicholas in Dutch. And I ride a white horse, you know, 'cause that's a smaller country and I don't need eight tiny reindeer. It was the Dutch that brought me to North America, to a town called New Amsterdam, that's modern day New York City. And I was loved here in North America, as I was back in Holland. But if you ever been to *Ne-ew Yo-ork*" pronouncing it with the proper accent you commonly hear, "You know they can do the words. The English speaking children mispronounced my name *Sinterklaas,* which means Santa Claus" stopping himself and correcting with "Saint Nicholas rather, and they started calling me what?"

"Santa Claus" the children in the audience call out but not yelling.

"Santa Claus," Saint Nicholas agrees explaining "Santa Claus really means Saint Nicholas. But a sad thing happened and in the 18th century, first part of the 19th century that's not long ago boys and girls more and more in North America people forgot why we really celebrate Christmas.

And one day, some folks came up to me and they said "Saint Nicholas, I'll tell you what, how about delivering gifts on Christmas Eve instead of December 5?" Well you can imagine the excitement honoring the birthday of Jesus. What an honor! But then they gave me an *extre-e-eme makeover!*" Pausing for a brief moment Saint Nicolas states in a not so happy tone "They had me dressed like an elf! That's the reason in 1822, Dr. Clement Moore wrote those words and you're familiar with them. He said he saw "*a little ol' driver so lively and quick, I knew in a moment it must be…*"

"Saint Nick" the children in the audience chime out finishing the famous quote for him.

Giving a puzzled look to the audience Saint Nicholas asks "Why was it, Dr. Moore had doubts in his mind whether it was Saint Nicholas here or not? Well I'll tell you, he knew I was a bishop, he was shocked to be seeing me dressed like and elf! Boys and girls do you realize that's the reason today we see on Christmas cards, on TV, or in films, there are leftovers of what I am wearing today? I'll explain it to you.

First of all, you know this funny hat I've got on" pointing to the hat that he wears, "It's called a bishop's mitre. Guess I don't have a hat box, I've got a mitre box, huh?" Chuckles come from among many in the audience as he continues without missing a beat. "Well you see that point right here? You remember the story of Pentecost, how the Holy Spirit descended on the friends of Jesus, and tongues of fire rested on their heads? This represents the tongues of fire. And this ribbon, on my left side, represents the Hebrew Scriptures, the Old Testament, foretelling the coming of Jesus. And on my right side, represents the New Testament, which revealed to the world that God kept his promise, and the word became flesh, and well, Jesus came into the world on Christmas. They're both enlightened, the Old Testament and the New Testament, by what? The Holy Spirit. Now you see what I'm wearing here? You're going to say, "hey that's a cape" but really we call it a cope. C, o, p, e. What they did, they shortened it up, and they put fur on it, and it became my furry coat. They changed my Pectoral Cross here, and that became my elf buckle. But finally, you know what this is?" he asks displaying his staff to the audience. "You've seen pictures of Jesus Christ, the good Shepard? He carries a staff that looks a lot like that doesn't he? This reminds a bishop, much like myself, that I'm entrusted with part of the flock that belongs to Jesus. This reminds me of the serious responsibility I have to follow Jesus, and be a Shepard to the people entrusted to my care."

Moving across the front of the stage, Saint Nicholas makes his way to the green sack he had laid down earlier. Laying his staff upon the stage, he pulls out an object while explaining "And that's the reason, no matter how I'm dressed today, I am always associated with *Candy Canes*" He turns to show the audience the large Candy Cane that he had retrieved from his sack. "That's the real reason" he reiterates again to make sure the point is clear.

Laying the Candy Cane on the opposite side of the stage from his sack, he turns towards the audiences and tells them "Now…I'm going to see if you've been paying attention. What happened to my hat? You know the triangle on my Santa cap, that's a bishop's mitre that fell over."

Looking over the audience, Saint Nicholas sees that they are a bit on the confused side. Without missing a beat, he pops to life with an idea. "I'll tell you what" he says "Maybe I'll do a pop quiz this way…I need one volunteer. One volunteer" he repeats, scanning the room. A young, roly poly, boy about the age of ten suddenly shoots his hand up in the air, to volunteer. "Come here, son!" Saint Nicholas exclaims. "Come up on stage" he gestures to the young boy helping him up to the stage. "Now let everybody see your hands and face and tell everyone your name" he tells him extending the microphone towards him.

"JACOB!" the young lad bellows loudly.

"Give Jacob a hand" Saint Nicholas says to the audience, which they do in kind. "Now, Jacob, I have a question for you…are you a professional model?"

"No" responds Jacob as he puts his hands into his pockets.

"He's going to have his debut today" Saint Nicholas says then tells Jacob "Now keep your hands out of your pockets...people will think you're a money grubber, for Heaven's sakes." This brings a chorus of laughter from all in the audience. As the laughter settles, Saint Nicholas continues, asking everyone "Now what happened to my cope, c,o,p,e? They shortened it up, put fur on it, and it became my furry what?"

"Coat" responds the audience.

"Coat" Saint Nicholas repeats. He sings *"It's beginning to look a lot like Christmas, everywhere you go. Take a look at the five and ten"* while making his way over to his sack to pull out a Santa coat. Showing it to the audience he states "Take a look at the stage, we have Santa Jake." Then he motions for Jacob to turn around. While doing so, Saint Nicholas positions himself so the audience's view of Jacob is obstructed, as he assists Jacob getting into the Santa coat.

Once the coat is on, Saint Nicholas turns Jacob around, moving out of the way to reveal Jacob, now dressed up in a Santa coat. He asks the audience to "Give him a hand!" and the applause for Jacob follows Saint Nicholas's request. Standing next to him, Saint Nicholas explains the similarities between the two of them. "Now you see what happened, see how... look at the likeness, even the color! What else changed?" he asks.

A small child in the audience responds "Your hat."

"Right" Saint Nicholas says. "It fell over and became what? A pointy Santa cap" he states again, going over to his sack to get another item out. Once again he walks over to Jacob, blocking him from the view of the audience, as he adds to the outfit. When Jacob is seen again, he now not only wears a Santa coat, but a Santa hat as well, which is sticking straight up in the air.

Saint Nicholas explains "See what we have here. We have a bishop's mitre. It fell over and became a floppy cap." At the moment he says this, the cap magically falls over into a floppy position. Turning Jacob towards stage left, he says "Show them. It became a bishop's mitre" as the hat straightens back up "Flopped over and became a floppy cap" as the cap once again flops back down. He repeats the process again for those sitting to the right of the stage so they can see it as well. After which Saint Nicholas once again calls for applause for Jacob.

As the crowd settles back down, Saint Nicholas moves on to the next change asking "What happened to my Shepard's staff it became what? Became my Candy Cane" he says handing Jacob the Candy Cane he laid down on the stage earlier in the program. Giving Jacob a once over, Saint Nicholas turns to the audience and says "You know what? What does he need to be an effective…a realistic helper?"

"Beard!" the audience replies.

"Are you ready?" asks Saint Nicholas of Jacob.

Jacob nods his head in acknowledgment.

Saint Nicholas heads back across the stage to his sack. Reaching it, he begins singing "*Oh, you better watch out, you better not cry, you better not pout, I'm telling you why…Santa Jacob's coming to town!*" Finishing the song with a little dance, Saint Nicholas one last time blocks Jacob from the audience and within moments, steps back to show off the young boy in full Santa costume, now complete with a beard.

"Give him a hand!" Saint Nicholas says, and as the audience does, he turns to Jacob and says "You know, Jacob, this is kinda scary. I feel like I'm looking in a mirror." The audience gets a kick out of the statement. "Okay, Jacob" he says to him "This is the moment of truth…let's hear that Ho, Ho, Ho!"

"HO, HO, HO!" Jacob bellows in a very convincing fashion.

"WOW!" Responds Saint Nicholas, taken aback. "He even sounds jolly! Give him another hand, everyone!"

As the audience applauds, Saint Nicholas goes over to Jacob and has him turn sideways, looking over to his left. Looking out into the audience, he announces "I need two more volunteers." He selects two young girls, no older than ten. Getting them on stage, he asks them their names. We learn that they are Baleigh and Martina. After they announce their names, Saint Nicholas gets the audience to applaud their efforts.

Placing them side by side, he instructs them to turn and face the same way as Santa Jacob is facing. Once into position, Saint Nicholas again for two more volunteers, getting their names and calling for applause for them. He does this a couple more times, until there are a total of eight children, of various ages and heights, in pairs, in front of Santa Jacob.

"Now see what we have here" he explains, "We have Santa, and Santa's imaginary sleigh, and eight tiny reindeer. But children do you know how to do a reindeer?" asks Saint Nicholas.

The children stand there for a moment not sure of what to do, until Saint Nicholas shows them. "Take your hands like this" showing them to spread their hands out wide, like making a number 5, with their thumbs in a straightened position. "Put them on your forehead, like this" showing them how to place their thumbs up next to their temples. "Those are your antlers" he explains. "Now when you fly" he continues "you have to bend your knees, so bob like this" showing them and encouraging them to imitate his movements.

As they get going into a rhythm, he comments, while still doing it himself, "Now see, this will teach you a valuable lesson in life, never volunteer for anything!" he says jokingly.

The audience roars in merriment.

Stepping back, Saint Nicholas summarizes "Now we have Santa Jacob. And his imaginary sleigh and eight tiny reindeer. We have all the reindeer we need right?"

The children in the audience respond with a low "No."

"What?" inquires Saint Nicholas. "What do we need?" he asks.

"RUDOLPH!" a bunch of children shout.

Pointing to a little girl who had tried to volunteer earlier, Saint Nicholas asks her "Would you like to be Rudolph, honey?" She starts to go up but stops suddenly, bringing this comment from Saint Nicholas "She's getting stage fright. Do you want to come up?" he asks again, encouraging her to do so.

With a lot of applause from the audience and a little coaxing from mom, this little girl, all the age of three or four, and shy to boot, makes her way onto the stage. Once in front of the other children Saint Nicholas asks for her name.

"Piper" she replies bashfully.

"Give her a hand!" Saint Nicholas calls out. The applause from the audience gives the little girl a big boost of confidence. Saint Nicholas starts to instruct her how to play reindeer, then stops. Looking out he asks the audience "Now wait a minute. If Piper is going to be a convincing Rudolph, what does she need?"

"A red nose" a little girl in the front row says in unison with the other children in the room.

"We'll fix you up, honey" he tells her as he reaches into his sack, pulling out a red nose which immediately starts to blink when he puts it on her nose. Getting the children who are playing reindeer to start bobbing, he begins to sing *"Rudolph the Red Nose Reindeer, had a very shiny nose..."*

Saint Nicholas encourages the entire audience to participate in the song through a couple of the main verses. When they all finish singing he bellows "GIVE THEM A HAND EVERYONE!"

The audience applauds as he asks for recognition for Rudolph. He dismisses Piper from the stage, followed by all the children who were playing the eight tiny reindeer, and finally Santa Jacob. Each group receives recognition and praise for coming up this afternoon to help Saint Nicholas.

Before Jacob can leave the stage, Saint Nicholas asks him for one last "Ho, Ho, Ho". Jacob has no problem bellowing it out once again in convincing fashion. As he helps Jacob take off the costume, he lets him know "Now I'll tell you what, Jacob. Since you are officially my helper, we'll let you keep the beard. Does that sound good?" he asks.

Jacob nods in agreement. He is asked by Saint Nicholas "Now how did it feel in there?"

"Good" replies Jacob with confidence.

"Weren't too hot?

"Nope"

"Boy, he's got the job!" Saint Nicholas declares, helping Jacob down off the stage with his beard still on. Saint Nicolas moves to center stage and stands silent for a moment to pause and reflect.

3

"I need one last volunteer" he says looking towards Heather who is sitting next to Nicholas in the front row.

Nicholas gives him a slight nod, at which Saint Nicholas points to Heather and beckons her to come up on the stage. Heather starts to go then hesitates, somewhat scared, but proceeds after getting a reassuring pat on the back from Nicholas.

Getting up on the stage Heather turns around as Saint Nicholas asks "Tell everyone your name."

"Heather" she replies.

Saint Nicholas sits down on the stage, he looks up at her and asks "Heather, do you ever play pretend?"

"When I was little" she tells him. "Not so much anymore."

"Okay, so you know how to play pretend?"

"Yes."

Saint Nicholas says to everyone "Let's pretend it's Heather's birthday. How would you like it, Heather, if we have a *great big, birthday party* in your honor? Would you like that?" he asks her.

"Yeah" she answers pretty excited.

Standing up and motioning to the entire audience, he continues "And I would invite everybody here to celebrate your birthday. Would you like that to?"

"Yeah."

"We would have lots of decorations, and lots of fun and singing, lots of cookies and fun food. Would you like that?"

"Yeah" she says now getting more excited.

"And lots and lots and lots of birthday…"

"Presents" Heather says, finishing Saint Nicholas's sentence.

"There we go" Saint Nicholas says now having not only her but the whole audience built up. Then he throws in the rub "But there would be one, teensy, weensy little catch, Heather. I'd invite everybody here; we'd have a wonderful time, but wouldn't invite Heather." He pauses to allow the point to sink in then asks her "How would that make you feel?"

"Very sad" Heather responds very disappointed.

"Sad" Saint Nicolas agrees. "Well you know what everyone, and Heather, now you know how Jesus feels when we celebrate the birthday, of Jesus, Christmas Day and leave Him *completely out!*" he tells them all motioning over all of them to make his point.

"I'm going to ask you to help me sing, Heather, the prettiest, happiest birthday song ever written to honor Jesus. We even have the Silent Night Chapel here that Wally and Irene Bronner erected to honor that song, Silent Night. Everybody!" Leading Heather, Nicholas, and the audience to sing...

> *"Silent night, holy night*
> *All is calm, all is bright*
> *Round yon Virgin Mother and Child*
> *Holy Infant so tender and mild*
> *Sleep in heavenly peace*
> *Sleep in heavenly peace."*

"Give yourselves a great big hand! Mormon Tabernacle Choir eat your hearts out! And give Heather a great big round of applause!" Saint Nicholas exclaims, as he escorts Heather off the stage back to her seat next to Nicholas.

4

As the audience settles, Saint Nicholas announces "Well, folks, I'm sorry to say, I've got to go. But before I leave, why am I so jolly at Christmas? Whose birthday do we celebrate?"

"Jesus!" the audience responds in a soft, reverent tone.

"I can't hear you!" Saint Nicholas says, placing a hand to his ear.

"JESUS!" the audience responds, still reverent but in a much louder roar than before.

"Now if you remember that for the rest of your life, you'll know my time here today would have been worth while" states Saint Nicholas confidently.

"You know in Holland what do they call me?" ask Saint Nicholas.

"Sinterklaas" is his response from the audience.

"You know me as…"

"Santa Claus"

"Which is just a mispronunciation of what? Saint Nicholas or Sinterklaas, huh. Some places they call me Kris Kringle. What do they call me in France? Pere Noel. In England, I'm known as Father Christmas. In Russia, they call me Grandfather Frost. In fact, you know what they call me now…in Turkey? Noel Bobble!" he chuckles, continuing his explanation "which mean Father Christmas. But no matter what I'm called by name, my spirit is still the same! I'm filled with the joy of the birth of Jesus, our Savior! I've got a little song and it'll express what I am trying to tell you"

Motioning to Julie, he has her turn on a small stereo tape recorder. A cute little jingle begins to play and Saint Nicholas begins to sing with a chorus of children singing in specific designated spots on the tape…

I'm old Saint Nicholas and everybody knows,
I always laugh with a Ho, Ho, Ho!
With a Ho, Ho, Ho! (Children)
Spreading joy where'er I go.
In Holland I'm called…
Sinterklaas! (Children)
In other places
Santa Claus! (Children)
They call me Sinterklaas and Santa Claus.

Because he's the children's friend! (Children)
Because I'm the children's friend!

The Babe in Bethlehem fills him with joy! (Children)
And now I share that "Peace on Earth" with girls and boys.

As the song goes into a small musical interlude, Saint Nicholas begins to clap, and the bells in his hands begin to jingle with the sounds of the season. "EVERYBODY CLAP!" he shouts. Putting his hand to his ears he continues his song…

Oh hark he hears the Angels sing! (Children)
And now I share the gift of hope this season brings!
I'm old Saint Nicholas and everybody knows,
I always laugh with a Ho, Ho, Ho!
With a Ho, Ho, Ho! (Children)
Spreading joy where'er I go.

In France they call me…
Pere Noel! (Children)
To others I'm just…
Kris Kringle! (Children)
They call me Pere Noel and Kris Kringle.

Because he's the children's friend! (Children)
Because I'm the children's friend!

The Babe in Bethlehem fills him with joy!
And now I share that "Peace on Earth" with girls and boys.

A second musical interlude follows, and Saint Nicholas calls for audience participation again. "This is the big wrap-up! Everybody clap!" he announces and leads the charge. It starts off small, then grows as he concludes his musical number…

In Holland I'm called…
Sinterklaas! (Children)

In other places...
Santa Claus! (Children).
In France they call me...
Pere Noel! (Children)
To others I'm just...
Kris Kringle! (Children)
In England you ask,
"Guess who Nick is?" (Children)
I'm just known as
Father Christmas! (Children)
In Russia they don't say...
"Nicklas" (Children)
Instead they shout out...
Grandfather Frost! (Children)
Though children of the world give Saint Nick—names,

His Spirit is still the same! (Children)
My Spirit is still the same!

"MERRY CHRISTMAS, EVERYONE!!!" he exclaims joyfully and wholeheartedly. "God bless all of you now and Merry Christmas!!!

5

Nicholas and Heather immediately stand and lead an overwhelming ovation for Saint Nicholas. As the ovation winds down, Saint Nicholas tells the audience "Now if you would like a picture with me, I'm going to ask you to form a line over here and go this way" motioning where they should move. "I'll tell you what" he adds "I won't even charge a modeling fee! What do you think of them apples? Merry Christmas everyone!"

"Would you like a picture with Saint Nicholas, Heather?" asks Nicholas.

"I would very much. But I don't have a camera" she responds.

"I think I have that covered" he tells her, reaching into his pocket to pull out his own I-Phone.

"I didn't know Santa Claus had an I-Phone!" she exclaims, astounded.

"Again the magic of being me" he responds.

They get in line and wait their turn for their photo op with Saint Nicholas. Within just minutes, it is their turn. Seeing Nicholas with Heather, Saint Nicholas smiles and asks as they walk up "So, Heather, did that help clear some things up for you?"

"Yes, it did. Though I still have some, inquiries, as Mr. Nicholas would say, on some stuff."

"Well, I'm sure that he will be able to answer them for you by the time your visit is done. Now, let's get a picture. Now stand a little bit closer here. Hold my staff, we'll have a staff meeting" he tells her. This produces a small giggle to a joke that she seems to get.

Nicholas snaps a couple pictures of her and Saint Nicholas. "Thank you Saint Nicholas. You have been a great help to my task today."

"You are most welcome, my friend. Hope that I'll see you again soon" responds Saint Nicholas.

"That you will. Come now, Heather" Nicholas tells her. "Still much to discuss, and our time grows short."

With that, Nicholas and Heather take their leave from the program center, heading back into the store to continue their discussion.

Creating

A

Persona

"His eyes, how they twinkled! His dimples, how merry! His cheeks were like roses, his nose like a cherry! His droll little mouth was drawn up like a bow, and the beard on his chin was as white as the snow."

- Clement Clarke Moore
"Twas The Night Before Christmas"
(1823)

Chapter 11

1

As they cross through the doorway of the program center, its doors slowly begin to close behind Nicholas and Heather. The first thing she notices: it is much busier than when she first arrived at Bronner's. Heather turns to make a comment to Nicholas about this. She stops herself short of doing so because the look on his face tells her his attention is focused elsewhere at this moment. How does she know this? Because it's the same look she has given her own parents on numerous occasions. Truth be told, she would be right.

Nicholas's attention is not on the busier crowd that has come to shop at Bronner's, but focused specifically on the sound of the closing doors of the program center. Though it is extremely loud in the vicinity, Nicholas uses his special talents to hone his hearing directly toward the sound of the doors closing. For him, that's all he hears. At the precise moment Nicholas hears the clicking sound of the doors, indicating they have completely shut, he snaps his fingers simultaneously.

The crowd disappears. Silence ensues.

Heather quickly notices that once again, it is only her and Nicholas. As they continue to walk, she comments, "Using your magic once again, Mr. Nicholas, so that it's easier for you and me to talk?"

"Indeed" he simply responds.

They walk silently until they wander into Section 6 of the store. Section 6 is decked out in Santa Claus figurines along a very long wall on the store's perimeter. The figurines are of all shapes and sizes and depict Santa Claus in various outfits. Looks from vintage to modern, various representations from other countries, even religious looks of him as Saint Nicholas, Bishop of Myra are represented. Heather studies each with the thought that every type of Santa Claus she, or anyone else, could possibly imagine appears to be represented upon this wall.

Nicholas watches as Heather studies all the variations of Santas displayed. Finally, breaking the silence of the moment, he remarks "A penny for your thoughts."

Turning her attention toward Nicholas, she studies him for a moment, looking back and forth between him and the ones displayed on the wall for comparison. "I kinda see the resemblance" she says to him, even though the way Nicholas is dressed isn't represented in anything that is displayed.

"Well then" he tells her. "Let's do a small review of Saint Nicholas's program and go from there. Shall we?"

"Sounds good to me" agrees Heather.

Looking around, Nicholas spies a candy cane lying on a small counter near the Santa wall. "Hand me that candy cane over there from that counter will you please?" he instructs her.

Walking to the counter, she picks up the candy cane and hands it to Nicholas. Upon placement it in his hand, a marvelous transformation occurs. The candy cane's stripes begin to peel and drop away, leaving it completely white. It begins to grow in length, narrowing into a tall staff. It changes color to match the staff Saint Nicholas had in the program.

Heather stands in awe as Nicholas's appearance begins to change as well. His beard becomes longer and more triangular. She continues to watch as the transformation continues. His coat lengthens before peeling from his arms, until it looks just like the cope that was described. The interior turns a velvety red color, while the exterior turns a beautiful soft white. Not only does the exterior of the cope turn white, so do Nicholas's clothes. As they lighten, whiten, they elongate, turning into bishop's robes complete with the draping over each shoulder.

A necklace, a cross to be precise, that Heather hasn't seen Nicholas wearing before, becomes very visible and slowly enlarges, until it is the size of the pectoral cross she had seen Saint Nicholas wear in the program.

The final touch of the transformation comes as Nicholas slightly taps his Bavarian hat upon his head. It immediately pops into a triangular bishop's mitre. "Behold" he speaks to Heather, "I am Saint Nicholas."

"Wow" is the only response she can muster.

"This is who I truly am" he tells her, giving her a moment to take it all in. He continues by asking "Now, you know me as whom?"

"I know you as Santa Claus" she responds, but quickly adds "But you look nothing like him."

"You are correct. Now think back to what you saw and learned in the program. Take it one step at a time."

Heather stands there for a moment and ponders. "Your cape!" she exclaims as that is the first thing she remembered.

"Cope" Nicholas corrects her. "What about it?"

"They put fur on it, and they shortened it to make it your coat."

"Exactly!" he says giving her a wink. At once Nicholas's cope shortens, fur appears on it in a blink of an eye, the bishop's robes become more form fitting and change color, until Nicholas now stands before her in his famous, and more well know red suit.

Nicholas quickly grabs his trousers so they don't fall down. Heather giggles at this, but quickly adds "Your cross becomes your belt buckle!" She no more than utters the phrase and the change takes effect.

As Nicholas composes himself, his beard once again shortens to what we are all used to seeing. "What is next?" he asks.

"Your hat" she says, explaining very correctly "It flops over and becomes your cap."

Again, the transformation takes place before her eyes. "And your staff becomes a candy cane" she adds quickly. The transformation of Nicholas from Saint Nicholas to Santa Claus is now complete. "Now you look like Santa Claus!" she tells him excitedly.

"The Santa Claus that you, and countless other children, have come to know and love?" he asks.

"Yes. This is how I'm used to seeing you as since as long as I can remember. And since I'm only eight years old, it hasn't been that long" Heather explains to Nicholas.

Nicholas gives a chuckle, explaining "Well, it took many years for me to obtain this look. What you see before you was due primarily to the work of three different men. These men were writers and artists who were gifted with imagination and knowledge. With a little Divine Influence from God, to help show them the way, they molded me from the Bishop I was to the persona of Santa Claus I am today."

Still paying attention to Nicholas, Heather moves over to a small cabinet resting next to the counter that had held the candy cane. Moving the contents on top of the counter out of the way, she hoists herself on top of it. Legs dangling, she puts her hands on her chin, elbows on her knees, and looks at Nicholas. In a cute, cheeky tone she says "Tell me more." Giving him a cheesy grin, she begins to swing her legs.

2

"Cute" he says to her.

"I'm listening" she tells him. Though her body language doesn't show it, the tone in her voice convinces Nicholas that she truly is paying attention.

"The first of these men" he explains "is an American author named Washington Irving."

"I don't know who he is" Heather immediately admits.

"I am certain that you do. He wrote a Halloween story that you might know called *"The Legend of Sleepy Hollow"*. It is a tale about a school teacher named Ichabod Crane who is terrorized by a headless horseman in a little village called Sleepy Hollow.

"Wait...I *do* know that story! I've seen the Disney cartoon of it. The horsemen had a "punkin" for a head! It's was scary, and I really don't like scary" she tells him.

"I don't blame you there, Heather" he tells her. "Well, prior to writing that famous and scary story, as you put it; Mr. Irving wrote a story entitled *"Knickerbocker's History of New York"* in 1808. Although in *his* story Saint Nicholas was no saintly bishop. Not even close to one. His version of Saint Nicholas was an old elfin Dutch burgher who was dressed in dark robes and smoked a clay pipe."

"What is a burgher, Mr. Nicholas?" asks Heather.

"A burgher is a Dutch or German term for a town dweller" answers Nicholas. In order to give Heather a better perspective of how different Saint Nicholas/Santa Claus first looked from what she is used to seeing, Nicholas goes to the wall of Santas and chooses one that's the closest to this representation. Picking it up from the shelf, he holds it for a moment, and then quickly replaces it upon the shelf from which he got it.

No sooner has he placed it back on the shelf, Nicholas morphs into the version of Saint Nicholas that he has just described to Heather.

Heather is a bit perplexed by this look. This version of Santa Claus is much smaller and thinner, for that matter, and the dark robes that he wears are not very festive for the holiday season. Even though his facial features are close to the Santa she is accustomed to and can see the resemblance, it is still a bit creepy, which she tells Mr. Nicholas without any hesitation or reservations.

He explains to her that this was a first attempt. Rarely do things we know and see in the world today become what they are from a first attempt. Sometimes it takes multiple tries to achieve the desired result. He continues to explain "Many of the details Mr. Irving used in his story to describe me are derived from the customs observed by the Dutch people who brought me with them to America, as you learned. In this version of me, I still delivered gifts to children, only I did so by dropping them down the chimney by means of a flying horse."

"But what about the flying reindeer and sleigh you use?" Heather inquires.

"They weren't thought of yet. They didn't come into being a part of my characteristics until 1821. It was in that year that an anonymous author published a little known poem entitled *"The Children's Friend"*. It was this poem that gave way to the notion that I used a sleigh and flying reindeer to deliver my gifts to children."

"But, Mr. Nicholas, the program didn't mention anything about Mr. Irving, or a poem" Heather insisted. "It mentioned a man named…"

"Moore" Nicholas adds finishing her thought.

"Yes! Mr. Moore is the man Saint Nicholas mentioned in his program."

"You are correct, Heather."

3

Nicholas explains "In 1822, Clement C. Moore wrote a poem for his children while on a sleigh ride home Christmas Eve. It was to be a bedtime story for them called "*A Visit from St. Nicholas*", but you know it better as "*The Night Before Christmas*."

"Is that the story that starts out with "*Twas the night before Christmas, and all through the house, not a creature was stirring, not even a mouse?*"" she recites word for word without missing a beat, as though she had it memorized.

"That it is" acknowledges Nicholas. "Sounds like you know it well."

"I do! Mom and Dad read it to me every year on Christmas Eve, just before bedtime. It helps put me to sleep so I can wake up early the next morning to see what you brought me under the tree!"

"Indeed. Well, Dr. Moore would have most likely read Mr. Irving's story as well as the poem and then expanded on those ideas to include all the characteristics I have today. Things like eight tiny reindeer, the sleigh, coming down the chimney to deliver gifts, and my overall appearance as you see before you now."

With the end of this statement, Nicholas looks to see a Santa on the wall that is a representation of the famous poem "*The Night Before Christmas*" and instantaneously changes his look from that of Irving's 1808 Dutch burgher version to that of Moore's vision of Saint Nicholas.

Once the transformation is complete, and looking more like the Santa Claus Heather is used to seeing, he finishes his explanation "Being Mr.

Moore was a professor, he knew of Saint Nicholas through his studies. Using this knowledge, he incorporated Santa Claus's gift-giving ways of the midnight deliveries and the filling of stockings hanging by the fireplace into his repertoire. And the rest, as the say, is history."

4

"So who was the third, Mr. Nicholas?" asks Heather.

"Well, ironically, being where you are and where I live currently, it is a Bavarian illustrator by the name of Thomas Nast who gave me sort of my final look, during the 1860's."

Looking at a display above them in one of the many alcoves throughout the store's sales floor, Nicholas gives a nod, and the display is transported directly behind him giving the effect he is looking for. It is a display comprised of a workshop, complete with elves building toys and a view of the North Pole from its window.

A list appears out of the blue as he tells Heather "Mr. Nast used Dr. Moore's description of me from his poem and then added his own touches to my persona. Things like me living at the North Pole, that I have a workshop there where I build toys with elves, and that I check a list of who's naughty and nice."

As he goes through and tells Heather what items Thomas Nast brought to his Santa Claus persona, he points out each, one at a time within the display behind him.

5

"Very interesting" Heather says to Nicholas.

"So, as you can see, what makes me Santa Claus is a combination of many factors. It is taking items such as my midnight visits and the leaving of items within stockings by the fire, which are factual, combining those factual elements with customs and traditions of the Dutch, and then combining all those aspects with the imaginations of authors and artists like Moore and Nast. You can even add the Coca-Cola Company to that list, as they improved upon Nast's concept of me, giving me more of a human image that you see today. It was the start, in my most humble opinion, of how I became commercialized with Christmas and the selling of products, which is a corruption of what I was to stand for."

"So, although Santa Claus is not bad, Saint Nicholas is a much better representation of what Christmas should be, due to the beliefs and history described in the program Saint Nicholas presented" Heather states emphatically.

"Heather" Nicholas says, with a tear in his eye, "You warm my heart with your words. You have been paying attention and are learning exactly what I was sent to teach. It would seem that my task is almost complete."

"Almost" Heather tells him. "You've told me how you as Saint Nicholas became the Santa Claus I know and love today. But that was through others creating who you are. You mentioned earlier that these men had gifted imaginations, and those imaginations where influenced by God."

"You don't miss anything, do you?"

"Nope" Heather says confidently. "So I guess the one question I still need answered is…How did you really become Santa Claus?"

6

Nicholas walks over to Heather and helps her down off the cabinet. As he places the candy cane he had been using, back upon the counter, the display behind him fades away, returning back into the alcove from which it came. He takes Heather's hand and leads her toward the South Entrance. As they walk, his Santa persona fades away and he reverts to the Bavarian look he's had since the beginning of their visit together.

Nicholas looks down at Heather and smiles at her with that "*droll little mouth shaped like a bow*" as described in Moore's poem. She looks up at him and smiles back. He knows that she completely understands Saint Nicholas's program as well as the history lesson he has given her about how Santa Claus came to be. This is the final piece to his task…explaining to her how he really became Santa Claus. For this, there is only one place at Bronner's to tell it…The Silent Night Chapel.

The Silent Night Chapel

"For me, music brings Christmas to life. Songs about the birth of Jesus transport me to the first Christmas."

- Ace Collins
*from "**Stories Behind The Best-Loved Songs Of Christmas**"*

Chapter 12

1

As the pair makes their way from the main store to the lobby area of the South Entrance, a banner, placed above a bin of pamphlets, much like the one in the West Entrance yet more modest, catches Heather's attention. She immediately lets go of Nicholas's hand to rush over to look at it.

On its left side is a beautiful picture of Wally and Irene Bronner standing in front of an arched path. The path leads to what she would describe as a church in the background. To the right of it she reads...

Visit... Bronner's
Silent Night Memorial Chapel
230 Steps from Bronner's South Entrance

"Is this where we are going, Mr. Nicholas? To see the Silent Night Memorial Chapel?" asks Heather.

"Yes it is, Heather" replies Nicholas. "You do not miss much do you? How did you know, if I may ask?"

"Call it a hunch" she smartly replies with a smile.

Nicholas chuckles at this. Before he can make any comment, Heather quickly asks "Is it really 230 steps once we exit here at the South Entrance?"

"I believe it is. But to quite honest I've never really counted it. Why don't you count it as we walk over there" Nicholas suggests.

"O-kay!" she exclaims happily.

Rejoining Nicholas they walk over to the exit doors and stop. As the doors automatically open in front of them, he looks over to her "Ready?"

"Yup!" she responds, wholeheartedly ready to proceed.

"Then here we go."

Taking the first step out the door, Heather confidently counts "ONE!" She continues to count out loud until she reaches 25, then continues her count silently, as they stroll across the desolate parking lot towards the chapel.

2

Exactly two hundred thirty steps, they reach a winding sidewalk path. Heather surveys the path in front of her. Just a few feet up the path, an iron arch has been erected. Across the top of the arch Heather reads the Old English style scripted words

Silent Night Memorial Chapel

Just below the scripted title, the main arch itself is a musical score of notes that represent the first few bars of the song "*Silent Night*".

On each side of the arch stand Victorian Style turn-of the-century lampposts, trimmed with pine garland and deep, rich, red bows placed directly under each lamp itself. Each lamppost is neatly placed in a small rock bed with perfectly manicured shrubbery.

To give Heather a better perspective of the beauty of this special place, Nicholas moves his hand slightly, causing the light of the day to dim to that of dusk. Reacting to this change, the lampposts at the beginning of the path as well as those lining the path to the chapel, ignite giving the area a very serene and divine feel.

"Shall we proceed?" he asks.

"Yes" agrees Heather. "It's so peaceful and quiet."

"As was intended" says Nicholas.

They make their way up the path, passing lampposts placed at alternating intervals; each wrapped in garland and topped with a bow like those at the beginning of the path. Beautifully manicured pines add to the landscape, aiding in that Christmas feel. Heather stops briefly to listen to the beautiful tune of "*Silent Night*" being played around them as they walk. She quickly discovers that the tune emanates from small speakers disguised as rocks that have been strategically placed along the path.

As they get closer to the chapel, Heather observes the multiple posted lyrics of the song. They are in a variety of languages, too numerous for her to count. "How many languages are here, Mr. Nicholas?" she asks.

"At last count, I believe the Bronner family has collected over 300."

"I never knew the world has so many languages!" she replies flabbergasted over this fact.

"Indeed there are" says Nicholas.

As they round the bend that lies at the front of the chapel, they come upon a rock bed platform. Centered in front of a magnificent lighted Christmas tree, rests a stunning life-sized Nativity made of unique whitened stone. Nicholas bows slightly to it as they pass; he is taken in by its simplistic exquisiteness. Heather is equally awestruck with it.

"Let us go inside" he suggests to Heather as they walk up a small flight of steps to the chapel's doors. Reaching out, Nicholas takes hold of the doors' handles pulling them open. The two enter quietly.

3

Heather looks around the very tranquil room. With the exception of the faint sounds of *"Silent Night"*, it is very still and silent. Peaceful as it was intended to be.

The interior of the room is divided into two distinct sections, a walkway and an enclosed glass chancel area. The walkway is lined with pews around the perimeter. There are stations placed around the room containing information about the composers of the song, the chapel itself, and a guest book for one to sign recording one's visit.

The glassed off chancel area is much more intriguing. Lying within is an alter area, surrounded by poinsettias, complete with a replica of Oberndorf's hand-crocheted filet alter cloth. Directly in front of the alter sit a couple of rows of pews; to the right, an Austrian-style Christmas tree and Nativity, and to the left, a memorial wreath with a guitar in its center.

Upon the alter rests a superbly carved Crucifix, made in 1818, next to a Bible opened to *Luke 2:1-19* (which relays the message of Christ's birth). The chancel area is finished by an enormous Advent wreath, star, and a crown hanging from the ceiling.

Nicholas stands there and observing Heather as she takes it all in. He, too, is fascinated by the chapel, thinking to himself how much it reminds him of the alter area of St. Nicholas Church. That is where he was on that Christmas Eve of 1818 when he first heard *"Silent Night"* sung, accompanied by nothing more than a simple guitar.

4

This is such a lovely place, Mr. Nicholas. What is so special about it?" inquires Heather.

"This place is special for two reasons" explains Nicholas. "First, this chapel is an exact replica of the chapel erected over the original alter site of St. Nicholas Church in Oberndorf, Austria. It was on this site where the church stood before being damaged by high waters of the Salzach River, that Pastor Joseph Mohr and Franz Xavier Gruber wrote and composed the most inspiring Christmas Carol of all time, *"Stille Nacht"* or *"Silent Night"*."

"This was mentioned in the program St. Nicholas presented" adds Heather.

"Yes, it was. This was the most beautiful song and to have been there to hear was truly an honor and most inspiring."

"You were there?!"

"Indeed, I was. And if you open your heart and listen very carefully, you can hear it as I did."

Closing her eyes, she stands listening intently. At first there is nothing. But after a couple of moments, she begins to hear a guitar and the song being sung. Though it is sung in Austrian, she completely understands it.

Heather opens her eyes, and the interior of the chapel has darkened. She sees the ghost-like figures of Pastor Mohr and Mr. Gruber, as well as those there on that Christmas Eve in 1818, including a younger looking Nicholas.

As the song finishes, Heather focuses on Nicholas himself. The lights come up, re-illuminating the room, and she watches as he ages into the person she has been talking with this day.

"Wonderful" she states simply, adding "You mentioned the chapel is special for two reasons. What is the second? And does this help explain how you really became Santa?"

"Let me address the second reason, for the explanation of it will lead to the latter inquiry" he says motioning for her to have a seat in one of the pews along the wall.

Sitting down, Heather gives him her undivided attention. Quite a feat for someone of eight, but she does so without a hitch.

"You see, Heather, Mr. Bronner visited the original chapel in Oberndorf in 1976. He was so inspired by it, he came up with the idea to have a replica built right here at Bronner's. Many years passed, but he was finally granted permission by Oberndorf's city government and the Visitor's Bureau of Oberndorf to do so; and in 1992 it finally became a reality. Now this is significant because upon its completion, the chapel was dedicated as a tribute to Austria's Christmas Gift to the world with the Christmas Hymn *"Stille Nacht"(Silent Night)*. More importantly this memorial was in thankfulness to God himself from Wally and Irene Bronner and family for all that He has given to their lives."

Heather sits there mulling over for a moment what Nicholas has just dispensed to her. Then she asks what would be the $64,000 question "What does this have to do with you actually becoming Santa Claus?"

Nicholas stands mute.

He then answers "Because I am thankful to God, as it was *God*, who made me Santa Claus."

Nicholas's

Life

"…the joy and meaning of Christmas only deepen as we grow older. We still find pleasure in exchanging greetings and gifts, and we still delight in the warm and colorful images of the holiday. But we perceive ever more clearly, as did Scrooge, that the true beauty and wonder of the season lie in the Christmas Spirit of giving of ourselves for others — the message of the Prince of Peace whose birth we celebrate."

- President Ronald Reagan
Message On The Observance
Of Christmas 12/23/87

Chapter 13

1

Heather just sat there. Mouth hanging open, and stunned for a second time today by what Mr. Nicholas has just divulged to her. She has serious doubts on this one. Then she stops to ponder upon it. It doesn't take her long to come to the conclusion that after all she has been told today, all she has witnessed with her own eyes for that matter, Heather knows deep down inside, now without a shadow of a doubt, this is so. It is as if she has seen it in *"The Sun."*

"God made you Santa Claus" reiterates Heather back to Nicholas.

"Yes" Nicholas responds simply.

"How?" she asks.

"How…how is a wee bit harder to grasp" admits Nicholas. He ponders now for a moment, thinking of the proper way to present this. Then it comes to him. "Throughout our visit on this day, you have come to learn how I became Santa Claus. You did so through the explanation of customs and traditions brought to this country by the Dutch, as well as through demonstrations using the imaginations of three very extraordinary, divinely inspired men. Would you concur?" asks Nicholas.

"What does it mean to concur, Mr. Nicholas?" asks Heather.

"It is a fancy way of saying you agree" Nicholas tells her.

"I understand" she quickly responds. "Then I agree, I mean concur" she says promptly correcting herself to match his vernacular.

Nicholas continues his explanation "Believe it or not, you have also been exposed to some actual facts about my true self in both. Though they have been so subtle you may not have recognized them."

Reaching deep into his jacket pocket, Nicholas pulls out a handful of snow. The fact he has had snow in his pocket all this time that hasn't melted doesn't intrigue Heather as much as the type of snow he holds. For this isn't your everyday, garden variety snow Nicholas holds, this snow is special. Heather knows what Mr. Nicholas holds in his hand is Christmas Snow. She knows this by the way it glistens in the soft light of the Silent Night Chapel, as well as by how white and pure it is.

Seeing her reaction to what he holds, Nicholas asks "You know what this is, Heather?"

"It's Christmas Snow" she tells him. "It is the type of snow that only falls on Christmas Eve and isn't seen any other time of the year."

"Very good" he tells her proudly. "Now you asked me how God made me Santa Claus."

"Yes, I would very much like to know how it became so" responds Heather sounding very much like a certain young eight year old girl of the 1800's she came to know today.

Nicholas states "To understand the "how", Heather, of me becoming Santa Claus through God's hand, you must come to know the facts about who I was back when I lived, back when I was Nicholas, Bishop of Myra.

2

Gently, Nicholas casts the Christmas Snow into the ceiling of the Silent Night Chapel. It hovers delicately in the air above them as the lighting within the chapel begins to dim simulating a calm, peaceful Christmas Eve Night.

Heather looks up in pure wonder as it begins to snow softly inside the chapel. She stands up from the bench where she is sitting to allow it to fall all over her. She turns to Mr. Nicholas and smiles. "This is the most beautiful thing I've ever seen" she tells him.

"Not as beautiful as what is to come" he assures her, as he directs her attention towards the glass enclosure of the chancel area.

Heather observes the pristine snowflakes adhere to each of the glass panels of the enclosure until each is completely frosted over, and she can no longer see inside. Looking back to Nicholas, he explains "All that I am, all that I have come to be as Santa Claus, came because of my deeds, and by God's Grace. Allow me to show you" he tells her as he motions in a semi-circular fashion, then back in a waving way that seems to cover the entire enclosure in front of them.

She watches as each of the frosted glass panels, with the exception of those in the doors at the center of the enclosure etch themselves into beautiful, stained glass style portraits. Each panel, enhanced by a very soft, Divine light, depicts Nicholas's life.

3

Heather stands there for a moment in awe of the great beauty and detail in the portraits within the windows. So in awe of it all, she scarcely knows where to begin, so she looks to Mr. Nicholas for guidance.

As she does, she is taken aback by his appearance. No longer dressed as she has seen him all day, he now appears like the St. Nicholas she met at the program earlier in the day, dressed in traditional ecclesiastical robes, wearing a traditional Bishop's mitre and carrying a staff know as a crozier. "Where am I to begin?" she asks.

Without a word Nicholas motions his crozier toward the left side of the chapel leading her like a good Shepard would to the first small panel. In the foreground Heather sees a small infant being cradled and loved by his parents while depictions of Patara lie in the background.

"Your birth?" she questions, certain that she already knows the answer to her own question.

"Yes. As you learned earlier on this day, I was born to a wealthy family in the city of Patara, which in that time was in Asia Minor. Now being accounts of such things weren't kept in that time, the exact date is not known though the experts place it sometime between 260 and 280 AD. Myself I would say it was in the year 265."

"Why's that?" she asks.

"No reason really. I just happen to like that particular set of numbers together."

"That's a good enough explanation for *me*" Heather lets him know, taking him at his word, while moving onward towards the next pane.

4

Within this second pane are depictions of Nicholas's life as he grows into a young man, being raised to be a devout Christian and to help and give to others. In one such depiction, Heather observes what looks like a ghost encompassing Nicholas. Somehow she has a feeling that this means something special and asks Mr. Nicholas what it means.

Nicholas's response to her is "Because my faith was so strong, and my devotion to God so great at such a young age, the Holy Spirit bonded with me in such a way that animated my spirit and soul, and drove me to become the person I am in life."

5

Heather nods her head showing she understands what he is saying and views the third pane of glass. Tragedy and death fill this pane of glass, as its story is of the epidemic that struck Nicholas's birth place of Patara, taking many lives, including those of his parents. Tears begin to fall down Heather's cheeks. "So sad" she mutters simply. "I can't even begin to imagine what it would feel like to lose my parents right now, and I am very sorry that you did."

"Don't trouble yourself with such things. It was difficult. It always is, losing someone you love, but I had my faith and knew they went to Heaven to be with Jesus. And as you know, I wanted to follow Jesus in the ministry. So do you remember the story you heard from the program today?"

Heather recollects for a moment then blurts out "The one about the young man that wanted to follow, Jesus?"

"Yes, that is the one. So if you look further down the panes of glass, you'll see that it is not as bleak and dark as it may first appear. I did exactly what Jesus had asked in order to follow him. I sold what I had, gave to the poor, and helped those in need, thus beginning my journey for God.

6

Heather gazes into the fourth pane in the room and becomes confused of its portrayal. Seeing this confusion upon her face Nicholas interjects "This pane represents me becoming the Bishop of Myra. I became so at a very young age and under some pretty unique circumstances."

"How so?" asks Heather.

"Well, one morning I was on my way to the church in order to pray. Upon my arrival I was asked by one of the wisest of bishops who I was. When I responded, telling him my name was Nicholas, he responded to me by saying...

"Nicholas, servant and friend of God, for your holiness you shall be bishop of this place"

He escorted me into the church and placed me upon the bishop's seat, where I was immediately consecrated the new Bishop of Myra. I later learned this wisest of bishops had heard the voice of God himself, telling him that the first person to enter the church on that morning, bearing the name of Nicholas, was to be the new bishop. Divine intervention...and it wouldn't be the last time in my life that it would happen."

7

"Now this fifth pane" explains Nicholas before Heather can get to it, "illustrates my pilgrimage to the Holy Land. I wanted to go walk where Jesus had, so that I could gain a better knowledge and understanding of

His life, passing, and resurrection. That way I could be a better service to Him."

8

Heather looks at the pane to the right of the doors, continuing the story, only to find it's simply frosted over. Paying it no mind for a moment, she looks to the one just past it, only to discover the same thing. She knows that all of the panes in the room etched into some sort of a picture. She witnessed them doing so. "This can't be all to your story, Mr. Nicholas. There has to be more" she tells him.

"There is more" he responds. "These panes are like a book. You wouldn't go to the last chapter of a book would you just to know the end?"

"I would be tempted in some cases, though I would still want to know what happened in between."

"Exactly, then seek and ye shall find, Heather. Might I suggest the pane at the end, the far right?" he asks her motioning her in that direction.

Taking his suggestion, she casually strolls down to that end of the chapel. The remaining panes reveal their etchings as she passes. Upon reaching the last pane, which would be like the sixth chapter of the story she gleefully shouts "I know what this one represents, Mr. Nicholas!"

"You do? Then please enlighten me with your wisdom on its representation" he implores her.

"This is where, under cover of darkness, you tossed bags of gold through an open window for a farmer's daughters, so they could be married instead of being forced into slavery or worse! It would become know as the first of your midnight visits" she tells him proudly.

Nicholas smiles at her. "You remember this very well from earlier. A great interpretation of this picture, and you are correct. Let me let you in on another trade secret about this tale. It is said that when I tossed those bags of gold through the window they actually landed in stockings that were hung by fire in order to dry. This rumor led to the custom of hanging stockings upon the fireplace for me to place gifts in them, helping to establish my reputation of being a gift-giver."

"Amazing!" exclaims Heather. "Never knew that was how *that* holiday tradition got started."

"Indeed" responds Nicholas as he watches her move on to the seventh pane.

9

Heather is very moved by this particular part of Nicholas's history. Within the pane it shows Nicholas standing in the way of a man trying to kill three men. She needn't ask what this means, as she understands that these men are no doubt innocent of whatever they have been accused of, and Mr. Nicholas is there to save them.

Other parts of the pane show Nicholas protecting sailors as well as saving and protecting children. Then she remembers from the program how St. Nicholas is always known as the children's friend.

10

Nicholas describes the eighth part of the story to Heather. As she looks, he explains "This one tells of a time when the city of Myra experienced a famine, during the year 311. I had learned that a group of ships in the harbor were carrying cargos of wheat destined for elsewhere. So being the person that I am, I went to those sailors and begged them to give but one simple measure of grain from each ship, in order to help the city. Do you know what they told me?"

"I would guess they told you no" says Heather.

"You would be right, Heather. They refused. They told me that it was all measured out, and it all had to be delivered to its destination. However, I told them if they were to do this. I promised them that God would make sure none of it was missing upon their arrival at their destination. Reluctantly they did as I asked and when they arrived at their destination it was as I said it would be. God made sure that it was all there as I had promised He would.

11

"A miracle!" exclaims Heather. I have never heard of one like that" she admits to Nicholas as she looks at the second to last pane. After studying it for a moment she asks "Is this when you were imprisoned for your beliefs?

Nicholas looks upon the pane of glass that shows him being tortured, beaten and threatened for his Christian faith. Yet the most important part of the pane is that of the foreground, showing that through it all he never wavered and stood fast in his faith, knowing that God would see him through.

"Yes, it was" he responded after reflecting upon the pane's meaning. "But as you have come to learn today, I sought not to die a martyr's death, but to be an example of how to live during such times of persecution, rather than die. I was what they would call a confessor."

"What is a confessor, Mr. Nicholas?" she asks.

"A confessor, Heather, is one who confesses his devotion in Christ publicly in times of persecution and remains faithful to Him despite being threatened with things such as imprisonment, torture or exile."

12

As Heather slowly walks to the final pane in the room, she thinks about what she has learned so far. It has been quite a bit, even for someone of her age, but she has understood it all. Giving the last pane a once over, she looks to Mr. Nicholas once again for explanation.

He explains "After I was released from prison some years later, I attended the first Council of Nicaea. This was in the year 325. There I and all the other bishops discussed and debated many ideals of the church, including the Holy Trinity. Unfortunately, none of my writings of that council remain today."

"How, then, do people know you were even there?" asks Heather.

"Well for one, I am listed among the attendees on the oldest of Greek accounts of the council. I also happen to be listed as being present there on five other lists. The other proof I was there was the fact that I helped to write what was called the *"Nicene Creed"*, though you may know it as the *"The Apostle's Creed"*, which is still said in churches to this very day."

"It sounds familiar" she tells him.

Taking pause for a moment, Nicholas opens his arms and says "This was my life. And a great one it was. I did many great things during my life, and it was all due to my faith in God, for it was through Him that all the things I accomplished were possible. There is no disputing this, and if I had to do it all over again, I wouldn't change a thing."

13

Heather listens to Nicholas's words as she takes another walk around the etched, frosted panes of glass, absorbing Mr. Nicholas's history one more time. She reunites with him at the doors leading into the alter area of the chapel. She notices they are frosted over, though they don't have any etchings on them depicting anything. Puzzled by this she asks "Why are there no pictures here on the doors?"

Nicholas stands quietly for a moment before answering. As he does, he carefully explains "You see, Heather, all good things must come to an end. One who lives, must at some point die. This is the natural way of things as it was intended to be. To some, dying is scary. As for me, I did not fear death. Do you understand why?"

"Because of your faith in Jesus" she replied.

"Precisely! You hit the nail on the head as they would say. I knew that I would have eternal life in Heaven because of my faith. What I wasn't privy to was that God had more for me to do for Him. You asked me earlier how I became Santa Claus."

"Yes, I did."

"Again, you have learned my history of becoming Santa Claus. You've also learned my history of who I was as St. Nicholas. With the understanding of both, you will be able to understand the "how" much better. And the answer to that lies through these doors. Are you ready?"

"Yes" Heather answers with assurance. "I am ready."

"Then allow me to show you first hand, little one" he says taking her hand in his.

Upon taking his hand, the doors which lead to the alter inside, open. What is inside is revealed. It looks nothing like what she has seen prior to the glass panes frosting over. All Heather sees is a very bright, yet soft, snowy white light in front of her.

She hesitates, almost afraid to go forward.

Nicholas assures her all is well with a firm grasp of his hand. This gives her the sureness she needs to continue on, and the two of them walk through the doors together. The doors softly close behind them. As they latch, the frosted etchings within the glass panes melt away, returning the interior of the Silent Night Chapel to its original form, leaving no trace that Heather or Nicholas were ever there.

The

Transformation

Into

Santa

"God never gives someone a gift they are not capable of receiving. If he gives us the gift of Christmas, it is because we all have the ability to understand and receive it."

- *Pope Francis*

Chapter 14

1

At first Heather is somewhat blinded by the intensity of the light while Nicholas navigates it as though it is second nature. The brightness lessens as the two of them walk together, and the distinct features of what Heather would describe as a bedroom, or bed chamber in Nicholas's time, come into view.

Though crude in its initial appearance, the chamber is actually very cozy and modest. As they draw closer, Heather spies a familiar figure lying on the bed, and he is barely breathing. It is Nicholas! How could this be when she is clearly standing next to him, holding the man's hand?! "Mr. Nicholas, where are we?! And what is going on?!" asks Heather in a mild state of panic.

"There is no cause for alarm, Heather. My apologies that I didn't give you fair warning of what was to transpire, as you have handled everything else today without much alarm. Let me assure you that it is quite alright. Now as to where we are, we are in my dwelling in Myra. However, though it is still December the sixth, we are actually in the year 343 A.D. What you see transpiring before your eyes are my final moments of life prior to my passing. Do not be frightened by what you see. Watch and behold the wonder of our Lord."

An air of calmness suddenly befalls them as the chamber illuminates. Exquisite rays of golden light glimmer down upon the dying Nicholas as three beautiful angels from Heaven descend upon him.

Nicholas smiles in wonder.

"Fear not, Nicholas" says one of the angels. "We have been sent to bring you home to God, the Father. With Him you will walk in His heavenly kingdom, along with His son and your Lord, Jesus Christ."

With his last breath of life, Nicholas utters *"In the Lord I put my trust!"* as he reaches his hand out to them.

Taking his hand, and with the aid of a second angel, Nicholas is lifted from Death, and with renewed strength, ascends with them to Heaven above, leaving his earthly shell behind. It is a sight that is both beautiful and sorrowful.

The remaining angel beams with admiration and turns her attention toward Heather and Nicholas. She asks "Is she to see what is to transpire and be blessed with the true meaning?"

"She is indeed" Nicholas responds simply.

"Then come, Heather, daughter of Harrison, and behold the wonder of God" the angel speaks.

Heather readily accepts the angel's invitation, walking over to her and extending her hand. The angel gently takes it, and she ascends with Heather and Nicholas into the golden light.

2

Instantaneously, Heather finds herself in Heaven. What she sees is simply astounding. She can barely begin to describe it. At first she thinks it is because of her young age, but then she remembers someone once telling her that everyone's perception of Heaven is going to be different. She didn't understand why at the moment. She just simply accepted this fact and would keep it simple if ever asked.

Heather looks up to the angel telling her "Thank you. It is very pretty here."

"You are very welcome, Heather. It has been a pleasure meeting you. Remember there is more beauty and wonder here to behold. I leave you in very capable hands. Farewell." Turning to Nicholas, she says to him "Always an honor to see you, Nicholas"

"The honor is mine" Nicholas responds in kind.

The Angel gives the slightest of nods, similar to that of a Japanese Monk, in appreciation before vanishing from view.

A brief moment of silence ensues. Observing her surroundings, Heather spies Mr. Nicholas off a bit in the distance. She sees an Elderly Gentleman approach him while he stands next to her. "So what is happening?" she asks him in a hushed voice.

"Ah, yes. Explanations are in order" he tells her. "What you are witnessing is an echo of the past. In a place such as Heaven, time as you know it, really has no meaning. Thus, what you are observing is the day I first met and spoke with my friend God. It was at this moment that he tasked me with being Santa Claus. I remember it well. It was as though it was only yesterday that we had this discussion. Let's watch and listen in shall we?" he suggests.

3

At first Nicholas cannot make out who is approaching him. Then as the Elderly Gentleman becomes clearer to him, he immediately knows who it is. Without a second thought on the matter Nicholas kneels as any penitent man would rightly do in the presence of God.

God smiles warmly and affectionately at Nicholas, "Rise" He simply tells him. As Nicholas gets to his feet, God extends his to hand to Nicholas "It is a pleasure and an honor to finally have you home, my friend."

Taking God's hand, Nicholas responds "The honor is mine, Lord. And I am thankful that You would have me."

Placing his hand upon Nicholas's shoulder God asks simply "Was there any doubt, my friend?" He gives pause for a brief moment allowing Nicholas to ponder. "If there was" he continues, not allowing Nicholas to speak, "then it should have been a fleeting one at best."

Nicholas nods in understanding as God continues his sermon.

"Nicholas, you have lead an extraordinary life, performed the most miraculous feats, given to those in need and given of yourself while neither seeking nor asking anything in return. Among all this, when in the face of horrible persecution, even death itself, never once did you waiver in your faith where others may have. You knew, without a shadow of any doubt, I would be there to help guide, comfort, and aid you. For this, you have my thanks."

Nicholas is humbled by God's statement to him. He responds in kind by telling Him "It is I who should be thanking You, and your son Jesus, without whom none of what I accomplished throughout my life would have even been possible."

God simply nods in acknowledgment.

There is a moment of silence that ensues between them. Nicholas is the first to break this silence by asking the straightforward question "How may I continue to be of service to You?"

"Funny you should ask, Nicholas" says God knowing full well Nicholas was going to ask this question even before he did. "I have a task for you that you, and you alone, are perfectly suited for. That is, if you are willing to accept it."

"As you know, Lord, I am always at your service" responds Nicholas.

"I know you are, my friend, but it is always polite to ask" says God.

"So it is" agrees Nicholas.

God explains "Nicholas, you were known for so many attributes throughout your life. Two of which make you a perfect fit for what I am tasking you with...that of your reputation of being a gift-giver, as well as being a protector and friend to children."

"It would certainly appear that I am a good fit for this task you ask of me. Wonder how that happened?" Nicholas asks with a smirk on his face.

"Am I that obvious?" says God smiling while rolling his eyes like he had nothing to do with what Nicholas speaks.

"At times you are not, Lord" replies Nicholas. "So what is the task at hand you ask of me?"

God gives Nicholas the full scope of his plan elucidating to him "You will become know as Saint Nicholas for you earthly deeds, and as such, you will continue on the path you were on before your death. Your appearance will change due to the times at hand and will be attributed to Washington Irving, Clement C. Moore and Thomas Nast, with a little influence from yours truly. Gaze into my eyes, Nicholas, and see my plan.

Nicholas gazes into the eyes of God and sees His plan. Nicholas sees how Washington Irving, Clement C. Moore, and Thomas Nast alter his appearance, with God's influence, from his Bishop look to what he will become. He sees what stories and traditions are created because of him, and just how many lives one simple person can touch.

As he sees all this flash before him, he hears the Lord's voice speak to
him...

> *"And though you will come to be known by many
> names, St. Nicholas, Pere Noel, Father Christmas,
> and many others, remember, Santa Claus to stay true
> to your core of giving, helping the poor, misguided,
> and the forgotten. And with the Spirit of Christmas,
> also known as The Holy Spirit, which you have so
> accepted into you heart, allow it to animate your soul
> and spirit, and it will give you the magic and
> communication of joy for which the Christmas Season
> is to be all about...the greatest gift, the birth of your
> Lord and Savior, Jesus Christ."*

Nicholas blinks and sees God looking down upon him. He notices
that his appearance has changed, and he now stands dressed as the iconic
Santa Claus that he will become known and loved for.

"Now go, my friend, it is time" says God to him.

Nicholas bows then turns to walk toward his new destiny the Lord has
set before him.

4

Heather looks to Mr. Nicholas and notices that he is dressed once
again as he was when they first met, as Santa Claus.

He smiles telling her "It is time for us to proceed as well."

Nicholas leads her directly toward the oncoming "echo" of himself.
As they meet, the "echo" and the real Nicholas walk side by side until
suddenly they merge into one. Still holding Heather's hand they descend
down what has the appearance of a flight of steps made only of light,
fluffy clouds.

Within just a few steps, they walk out an invisible doorway right into the main aisle of the alter area of the Silent Night Chapel and out its doors from where they first entered not so long ago.

Walking towards the exit, Nicholas lays a finger aside of his nose, and they walk through the exit door of the chapel out into the night.

Looking For Christmas

"Christmas in Bethlehem. The ancient dream: a cold, clear night made brilliant by a glorious star, the smell of incense, shepherds and wise men falling to their knees in adoration of the sweet baby, the incarnation of perfect love."

- *Lucinda Franks*

Chapter 15

1

Walking out of the Silent Chapel, Heather becomes conscious of the fact that there is something quite different at play here. Though she should be startled, maybe even a bit scared by this fact, she is as calm as can be. Mr. Nicholas is with her, and winding up in different places or times has been but commonplace from the start. Why should it be any different now?

It was daylight when they entered the chapel, but now night has fallen and it is black as pitch. Looking with the help of the light given off by the chapel itself, she can see that it had just recently snowed, the fresh powder glistening in the light.

Nothing else is visible. No light from Bronner's, which is only a mere 230 steps away; nothing from the highway which runs out in front of the Silent Night Chapel just as close if not closer; not even a single light from the city of Frankenmuth itself which lies just down the road. It is downright quiet and calm.

That silence and calmness make Heather think of the lyric from "*Stille Nacht*" that she had heard St. Nicholas sing earlier in the day. It echoes in her mind that *"all is calm"*. Yet before she can finish the thought Mr. Nicholas beckons "Come, Heather. The time is near, and you do not want to miss it."

"Miss what?" she asks following him out into the snowy darkness.

"You will see. All I will tell you is that it is the most joyous occasion that you will ever witness."

Dashing through the snow to catch up with Mr. Nicholas, Heather finds the snow is a tad bit deeper than she originally thought. It is difficult to navigate with her short legs, and she struggles to keep up with Nicholas who navigates through it with great ease. As she finally catches up with him, the snow seems to thin, beginning to feel more like solid ground with a different consistency to it…the consistency of sand.

Before Heather can even think to ask Mr. Nicholas what is going on her attention is suddenly sidetracked by the unexpected appearance of a bright star fixed within the night sky. Gazing deeply upon it, she thinks it is the brightest, most beautiful star that she has ever seen, admiring how its luminance bathes their surroundings with a very soft, angelic light.

Heather reverts to her earlier thought of the song "*Stille Nacht*". She can now hear the remaining part of the lyric she was thinking of earlier echo in her mind about how "all is bright". It truly is a "Silent Night". And she is about to find out more than she can possibly ever imagine.

2

Now that there is light to see by, Heather scans her surroundings to find that she is walking through an actual desert. Nicholas looks over at Heather and knows she is perplexed once again by her situation. Though he knows it isn't really bothering her, he asks "Do you know where we are?"

"I know we are in a desert, but I'm not sure which one or where" responds Heather.

"Fair enough" says Nicholas. "Then do you know what the significance is of that star in the sky you are so admiring?"

Heather thinks for a moment, knowing that is has some significance. What, she can't think of and simply responds, "No."

Instead of giving her the answer and wanting her to think about it, Nicholas tells her "Let me give you a hint." He stops in his tracks and clears his throat with a great intensity. Then he begins to sing in a deep voice…

"Star of wonder, star of night.
Star with royal beauty bright.
Westward leading, still proceeding.
Guide us to thy perfect light."

Heather recognizes what Nicholas sings is part of a Christmas carol, one that she knows she has heard numerous times over the years. The name of it escapes her at the moment, but she knows, that it is about the star that leads the Wise men to Bethlehem where Jesus was born.

It hits her like a ton of bricks and says to Nicholas "That is the Star of Bethlehem!"

"Indeed it is" responds Nicholas.

"Then we must be on our way to Bethlehem?! Am I right?!"

"You are right, Heather. And we are almost there as we speak" he tells her.

"Then are we…" he thought silenced by the mere motion of Nicholas bringing a finger to his lips.

Walking silently, the two of them spy a light off in the distance. It quickly grows brighter as the distance between them grows shorter with each step they take.

3

Within a tick, they are upon a very simple stable, above them the Star of Bethlehem shining ever so bright…and then it happens. A divine light emanates through every open crack, window and crevice in the stable, lighting the area around them up with blinding, pure white light.

Then nothingness falls while silence ensues.

They then hear the cry of a new born baby. "Is that…?" Heather asks, stopping in mid-sentence, knowing the answer to her own question suddenly.

"It is" Nicholas confirms to her. "Behold, the true meaning of Christmas" he tells her as he opens the stable doors.

Inside, the first thing Heather lays eyes upon is a babe, wrapped in swaddling clothes, and laid in a manger. It is the new born king, Jesus Christ. He is the most beautiful baby she has ever laid eyes upon and ever will for that matter. He, for lack of any other word, is simply "perfect".

Nicholas and Heather stand at the edge of the doorway until they get a nod of acceptance to enter from Mary and Joseph. Though they aren't dressed in the clothing of the period, Mary and Joseph see them as though they were in such attire, and remain silent as the two enter.

Reaching the Babe of Bethlehem, Nicholas stands in awe at the sight of our infant Lord much as he did the first time he bore witness to this. It was a sight firmly etched into his memory, one that he could never tire of reliving. Looking at Heather, he observes that she is just as taken in by the sight as he is.

Nicholas takes a knee, then removes his Santa cap and bows his head before the Christ Child. Seeing this, Heather mimics Nicholas's actions; taking a knee, bowing reverently before Him.

The moment is perfect.

In a very silent yet honored voice, Nicholas explains "This...this right here...is the true meaning of Christmas. It is what the season is all about. It is not about what will be found under the tree on Christmas morning, what we need to go out and buy someone, or even the whole commercialization of it all. And even though I was meant to be a part of Christmas, it has not one thing to do with me either. It does, however, have *everything* to do with the birth of our Lord and Savior, Jesus Christ, the greatest gift ever to be given. If you take one thing from our time today, may it be this."

Heather nods, understanding what Mr. Nicholas has spoken to her. Acting how all young kids do around infants, Heather goes to touch the Christ Child, though stops in midstream. She looks up at Mary, and remembering her manners, politely asks "May I?"

Mary responds with a simple nod of acceptance.

Situating herself, Heather reaches in and gently touches the face of the baby Jesus. Such a pretty baby, she thinks to herself as she smiles at Him. His little hand comes loose from His wrapping, and instinctively He grabs her finger. She looks deep into his beautiful eyes.

Precipitously, a glow of light encompasses Heather, and she grasps the truth of it all. Everything that she has been shown, spoken to her, and demonstrated throughout this day with Mr. Nicholas is confirmed. No longer is there any doubt or question in her mind. Then she hears a voice speak to her...

> *"The core of Christmas Heather can be summed up in four simple words. They are Peace, Hope, Love, and Joy. Remember these words and you will never falter. Go now with Nicholas and rejoice in the reason for the season."*

With this being spoken, Heather suddenly hears the sound of the Glockenspiel Tower and its thirty-five bells from the Bavarian Inn in the distance. She breaks from her euphoria to see she is no longer kneeling before the Christ Child in Bethlehem but with Mr. Nicholas, kneeling in the snow before the stone nativity located right outside the Silent Night Chapel.

The

True Meaning

Of

Christmas

"Love is what's in the room with you at Christmas if you stop opening presents and listen."

- Author Unknown
Attributed to a 7 year old named Bobby

Chapter 16

As the chimes from the Glockenspiel diminish and grow faint in the distance, Nicholas realizes that his time with his new friend Heather is at a close. His task that he was set upon now completed, it is now time to bring reality back into play and send her forth with the knowledge she has gained, in hopes that it will be imparted and mentalities changed.

Standing, Nicholas takes his cap and brushes the snow from his knees before replacing it back upon his head. "Time for us to be getting back, Heather, our time together is now at an end" he says to her as he extends his hand to help her back to her feet.

Looking up at Nicholas, she accepts his hand and hoists herself back onto her feet. Brushing the snow off her knees as well, she looks around to gain her bearing on where and when she actually is. This being stunned for a third time this day is very wearing on a person.

Heather follows Nicholas silently back down the path until they reach the iron archway at its beginning. She stops as Nicholas steps off the sidewalk and into the parking lot. He realizes in an instant she has done so. Turning he ask "Is there something wrong, Heather?"

"Nothing is wrong. It's just that I have a couple of questions or inquires, as you have often said today, on what I've learned."

"Then ask away child. But let us talk and walk as we do. Remember we do have 230 steps before we are back at the South Entrance of Bronner's, so you will have more than ample time to get the inquires you have resolved" Nicholas tells her.

She smiles and continues to follow him back toward Bronner's. Thinking for a moment she says "You've mentioned a couple of times during our visit that Christmas has become com...mer...cial...ized, commercialized. And you, as Santa, have been tied to that.

"Yes, that I have, and it is unfortunate that it has become so. Seemingly it gets worse from year to year. What about it?"

"I understand what you are saying but am confused by if it was God's will to have you be a part of the season, and from what I learned today, He did so at great lengths, wouldn't He see this coming, being He is all knowing?"

"You are a very bright and perceptive young lady, Heather. To answer your inquiry you have to understand that our Lord works in mysterious ways. He, like most, is intrigued by the way things can tend to play out. And knowing Him as I do, I am sure it was His intention to let it play out as such. There are always lessons to be learned in what He does. And when He feels we have learned that lesson or have gone astray from His wishes, then He intervenes to get us back on track. Hence, that is why I was sent to you on this day, to convince you that Santa Claus really exists, what His true purpose is, and the true meaning of Christmas."

"I see" she tells him. "I heard a voice while Jesus was holding my finger, telling me that the core of Christmas could be summed up into four simple words."

"Indeed they can" Nicholas tells her. "Do you remember what they are?" he asks.

"Yup!" she exclaims. "They are Peace, Hope, Love, and Joy."

"Excellent! Remember them well, Heather, and you will never falter just as God told you."

"I will. But do each of them have a specific meaning, other than just simple words that they are?" asks Heather.

"They do indeed. Peace represents the Spirit of Christmas which is actually one and the same with the Holy Spirit. With it one can do miraculous things. Then there is Hope, which represents the Joy of Christmas. With a little Hope one can accomplish a great many things. Next we have Love, which is the true Heart of Christmas. Love for others, such as family, friends, but more importantly, for those who are less fortunate, misguided and forgotten. Finally, there is Joy. Joy, though also a part of Hope, is representative of what the true meaning of the season is…the birth of our Lord and Savior, Jesus Christ. So again remember these words and their meanings, and you will never lose sight of what Christmas is supposed to be."

Nearing the South Entrance of Bronner's, with just a few steps of the 230 left to go, Heather inquires on one last thing. "Why was I chosen, Mr. Nicholas? And what is it that I can do, since I'm only one person?"

Nicholas ponders for a moment before answering "Why you were chosen is known only to God. I could only guess as to why He chose you versus someone else. My instincts tell me it was because you are true of heart, open minded, and much like the young Virginia of her time. As to being only one person, don't let that trouble you. It has been said, in and throughout history, that one person can make a difference. If you need proof of that, look no further than to Jesus himself. With the knowledge that you now have, in time, I'm sure you will impart it to another. They will agree and in turn will impart it to someone else. Before long, many minds will change and things will hopefully return to what they should be. Time will tell. Do you understand what I am saying?"

"Yes, I do" says Heather.

Upon reaching the doors to the South Entrance Nicholas stops and composes himself. He looks at Heather and says "Are you ready?"

Heather looks at him and smiles. "Yes, I am ready" she tells him.

"Then here we go" he tells her.

The two of them walk in unison activating the automatic doors. Once they have stopped moving, the two enter the building ready to put things back into perspective.

The

Santa Swap

Back

"I will honor Christmas in my heart, and try to keep it all the year."

- Charles Dickens
"A Christmas Carol"
(1843)

Chapter 17

1

Nicholas and Heather walk over to the exit of Santa's Workshop which is just inside the South Entrance's foyer. Peering in they see the display Santa that swapped with Nicholas, doing his due diligence, portraying Santa Claus like it was second nature to him.

As he finishes up with a young lad, he looks up ready to greet the next child in line which just so happens to be Heather. As she walks up, toward him, Display Santa catches a glimpse of Nicholas just inside the exit but not enough to draw the attention of anyone within the workshop area. He inconspicuously puts a finger aside of his nose and gives a nod to Nicholas to indicate that he is ready.

Nicholas turns to Heather, who is again amazed at what her eyes tell her. "How can I be there with the fake Santa and standing next to you at the same time, Mr. Nicholas?" she asks knowing as soon as she has spoken the question she really already knows the answer.

"Magic" Nicholas simply responds. "It is all a very good illusion that will allow us to make the swap back unnoticed by anyone around. So without any further ado…" he says giving her a wink of his eye and a slight wave of his hand over everyone in the room.

2

Once again, with the exception of her and Nicholas, everyone in the room freezes in place as time is once again stopped, just as it had been earlier when they embarked on their visit. "Shall we proceed?" he asks.

"Yes, we shall" she replies in a very proper accent.

Nicholas leads them through the workshop area and upon reaching Display Santa; the "Illusion Heather" disappears from the scene. Once completely out of the picture, the Display Santa stands and extends his hand to Nicholas.

Returning the gesture, Nicholas shakes the Display Santa's hand "I thank you for your time and aid, Santa Claus, and I hereby relieve you, sir."

"You are most welcome, Nicholas. Thus, I am so relieved. If I can be of service again you know where I'll be."

With this, the Display Santa turns and begins to walk towards the wall. Nearing the wall, it once again becomes transparent. Display Santa makes his way through it, back across the still crowded store, through displays and people, like a ghost. Everyone is still unaware of what is going on.

Upon reaching a certain point just below the ledge, Display Santa turns and waves to Heather and Nicholas. She watches again in amazement as he leaps into the air performing a back flip and landing perfectly upon the ledge in his sitting spot. As he assumes his original position upon the ledge, his human facade breaks away and reverts to its original plastic form.

3

With Display Santa now back in place, Nicholas sits down in his chair. In doing so, the wall behind them returns to its original solid state. He motions Heather over and hoists her up onto his lap just as the "Illusion Heather" had been moments ago.

Nicholas goes to speak, but his thought is interrupted by the sound of Heather's stomach growling something fierce. "It sounds like you are pretty hungry there, young one" he says to her.

"Yeah, it is about that time when we usually eat dinner" she tells him.

"Well then, one last gift for you before you go" he tells her pulling out a gift card (wrapped with a bow) from his right hand coat pocket.

"What is this?"

"This is so you and your family can enjoy dinner together, since I kept you from them all day."

"Thank you, Mr. Nicholas. Where is it to?" she asks.

"It is to a little place, just down the street, called the Bavarian Inn. They have the best all-you-can-eat chicken dinners with all the fixings. When you get there, tell them Dorothy sent you and hand them this card. They will know what to do as it has all been arranged."

"That sounds so good! Thanks again, Mr. Nicholas."

"No, thank you, Heather" Nicholas responds. "Now it is time for me to bid thee farewell."

Tears begin to trickle down Heather's cheeks as she is sad to have to say goodbye to her new found friend. "Will I see you again, Mr. Nicholas?"

"I am sure of it. Now, dry your eyes. Visits with St. Nicholas, or Santa Claus, are to be joyous! Not sad. We don't want these other children to get the idea that your visit was bad, now do we?"

"No, we wouldn't" she tells him as she uses her sleeves to dry her eyes. Getting into character for Mr. Nicholas, she looks at him and tells him "Thank you, Mr. Nicholas. For everything…it has been a pleasure."

"The pleasure has been mine, Heather. And you are most welcome. Remember what you've seen, heard, and learned here on this day. Hold it dear to you always. And when others question or have doubt, let them know the truth of it all."

"I will" she assures him.

Nicholas gives her a hug and tells her "Okay now. Follow my lead here" and with a snap of his fingers the people in the workshop area return to normal.

"HO, HO, HO!" Santa Claus exclaims mightily. "Santa will see what he can do about filling you Christmas list, young lady" he says to Heather as he reaches down into his sack at the side of his chair, handing her a candy cane. "You have a very Merry Christmas!"

"Merry Christmas to you as well, mister…I mean Santa Claus!" she replies as she jumps down off his lap and walks down the path toward the exit.

Upon reaching it, she pauses to look back. Mr. Nicholas is already in conversation with another young child, listening to his Christmas wishes.

Nicholas, sensing this, looks over at her for a brief moment and smiles as only St. Nicholas can. She waves joyfully back and returns a whopping smile to him. Heading out the exit of Santa's Workshop, she relishes the fact that this has been a joyous and special day. One that she knows in her heart she will never forget.

Fun & Truth

In Shopping

"Then the Grinch thought of something he hadn't before.
Maybe Christmas, he thought… doesn't come from a store.
What if, Christmas, perhaps…means a little bit more!"

- Dr. Suess
"How The Grinch Stole Christmas"

Chapter 18

1

Heather is just a few steps outside the exit to Santa's Workshop back inside the store's South Entrance, when she catches a glimpse of her parents sitting over in a seating section adjacent to the South checkouts. Gleaming with excitement upon seeing them, she yells across the checkout area "MOM! DAD!" as she makes a quick beeline to them.

"Well, there she is!" says Harrison as she wraps her arms around him to give him a big bear hug. "Your mother and I were beginning to wonder. It feels like we've been sitting here for hours waiting for you. You and Santa Claus must have been carrying on one heck of a conversation to be gone this long!" he says to her in a very exaggeratory fashion.

"Really, Harrison" says Audrey kind of scolding him with her tone and shaking her head that he would even say such a thing.

She is so glad to see them. But then she notices a large shopping sack, bearing the Bronner's logo, sitting beside her mother. In it are the special decorations that Mr. Nicholas had spoken about, even going so far as to give them a gift card so that they could go buy them while she spent time with him. Heather can't help but feel just a tad bit bummed out and she wants to cry. After all she has come to Frankenmuth to spend the day with her parents and shop here at Bronner's, the world's largest Christmas store. Instead, she spent it all with Mr. Nicholas, and now it is time to leave.

"I'm sorry, dad," apologizes Heather. "Mr. Nicholas and I got to talking about how he is truly Santa Claus, Saint Nicholas rather, met a St. Nicholas and saw his play over in the program center here on how St. Nicholas became Santa Claus, learned about a girl named Virginia and how she wrote an editor at "*The Sun*" asking if there truly was a Santa Claus, went to the Silent Night Chapel out back and learned its history as well as Mr. Nicholas's true history, saw Mr. Nicholas die and go to Heaven, actually went to Heaven and saw how God turned him into Santa Claus, went to Bethlehem and saw the birth of Jesus, and learned what the true meaning of Christmas is, and while I was spending the day with Mr. Nicholas learning all of this, you guys were shopping without me, and now it's time for us to go and who knows when we'll come back here!" rambles Heather in a long-winded rant, bursting into tears as she finishes.

"O-o-k-a-a-y" Harrison and Audrey say together as they look at each other, completely dumbfounded by what Heather just blathered on about. They stare at each other in silence allowing Heather to calm down a bit and catch her breath. Knowing what the other is thinking, they come to the same conclusion as to what is going on. Simply put, it is nothing more than an overexcited and overwhelmed eight year old who just visited with one of the most realistic Santa Claus's either had ever seen.

Knowing that they can't enjoy the rest of their day at Bronner's with their daughter in this state, Audrey lightly pats the empty chair next to her and says "Come over here and sit with me for a minute, Sweetheart."

Heather begrudgingly accepts the invitation dragging her feet as she walks to the chair, all the while hanging her head low in shame. As she takes the seat, her mother hands her a tissue telling her "Here. Now dry your eyes and let's talk about this."

"Okay" she says taking the tissue from her mom. She wipes her eyes and blows her nose so hard that it sounds like a small trumpet. Audrey smiles, shaking her head over all this drama which, since she knows her own daughter, probably amounts to nothing at all.

Audrey waits patiently for Heather to settle down. When she has, Audrey asks a simple question to help put things back into perspective. "Heather" she says, "What time do you think it is?"

Heather immediately chimes back "It has to be at least past 7 o'clock."

"What makes you think that?" asks Audrey.

"Because just before Mr. Nicholas and I came back from the Silent Night Chapel I heard at least seven chimes from the bell tower from down the street."

"I see" says Audrey going along with this fairy tale. "Well then, would it surprise you to learn that it's not past seven?"

"It's not?" questions Heather, perking up somewhat by the news of this.

"Nope, not even close to seven."

"Then what time is it then?"

"It's only 12:25 pm" Harrison responds as he looks at his watch.

A flummoxed look comes across Heather's face at the sounds of this.

Seeing that this needs a little more explanation, Audrey points out "Heather, we arrived at Bronner's right around 11 o'clock this morning. We came in and got you all set up to see Santa, and then started looking around before you got hungry. If you remember, we were on our way to the get something when they called your group to see Santa. We did a 360 and went straight to Santa's Workshop and got in line, which I will admit did moved rather quickly for as busy as it is in here today. When we got up to Santa, with one child ahead of you, we told you we were going to wait outside the exit so that you could have a nice visit with Santa on your own, which is what you told us you wanted to do before we left this morning. When we went outside Santa's Workshop it was about twelve, noon."

"But you guys went shopping without me!" Heather exclaims to her parents pointing at the Bronner's shopping bag that sits right in front of them clear as day.

"We did some shopping, Heather" admits Harrison. "There have been some special decorations that your mother and I have wanted for our home for quite some time. It just happened that they were located in a section right next to Santa's Workshop. So while your mother waited I went and snatched them up. I was about to get up and take them to the car when you came out."

Putting her mind to it, Heather thinks for a moment. Then the "look of a light bulb going on" comes to her once distraught face. "So, I was only with Santa Claus for, like 25 minutes then, not all day?"

"Correct" her parents tell her in unison.

"And the only shopping you did was for the special decorations, and that was only because they were nearby. So are we still going to shop?"

"That we are" says Audrey.

Before she can say anything her father adds "You have to remember, kiddo, a visit with Santa Claus seems actually longer than what it really is. It's part of the magic of Santa that only he seems to have."

"*Magic*" thinks Heather to herself.

Her father just hit the proverbial "*nail on the head*". Of course it is magic! She should've known what was going on the minute her mother told her what time it was. Mr. Nicholas is behind this! After all, he is Santa Claus and after everything she has witnessed today this should come as no surprise. Stunned yet again! "WOW!" exclaims Heather aloud. It is the only response that comes to mind.

2

"So, kiddo, you ready to do some shopping?" her father asks.

"Definitely!" Heather responds practically jumping out of her seat ready to go. "But aren't you going to take that out to the car first?" she asks, pointing at the shopping bag filled with what they have already purchased, knowing full well it is going to take a few minutes to do so.

Seeing that look settle on Heather's face, indicating she really wants to get going, (and wasn't going to be happy waiting any longer than she has to) Audrey looks over at Harrison and says "You know we can just put the bag in the bottom basket of the cart instead of taking it out to the car. There will still be plenty of room for anything else we might want to get, and if not, we can always grab another cart. Then when we're all done, we can take everything out to the car all at once. It will save making two trips, and we can *get going*" she hints to Harrison.

"I see your point, and that sounds like a very good idea to me" agrees Harrison, understanding what Audrey was trying to convey to him. Picking up the bag, he situates it in the bottom basket of the cart. As he does, Harrison says "Might I make a suggestion?"

"Sure" Audrey and Heather respond in unison.

"If my memory serves, it seems to me we were on our way to the Season's Eatings Snack Area to get something to eat. That was, of course, before someone's group was called to see Santa. I don't know about you, ladies, but I think *that* should be our first order of business before we get into shopping."

"I think that is an excellent suggestion, honey" agrees Audrey. "What about you, Heather?"

"That's a great idea, Dad! I'm starving! I know I can't make it until later after we are done!" Heather adds.

"Then I suggest we head over there before you waste away! We wouldn't want that now would we?" he states to Heather, leaning over to give her a great big hug.

3

Slowly, but surely, the family makes their way back toward the Season's Eatings Snack Area, stopping every so often along the way to look at different things that happen to catch their eyes. More often than not, they stopped to look due to what caught *Heather's* eye. Harrison and Audrey half expected this because this is Heather's first trip to Bronner's, a store so immense there is quite a bit to see and take in.

Even with all the stopping they did to look at things, they were still back at the snack area within a few minutes. Getting in line, which was just a tad longer than before but moving right along for as busy as it was, Audrey asked Heather "So what are you going to get to eat, sweetie?"

"I don't know. What do they have other than hot cocoa and pretzels? I already had those with Mr. Nicholas earlier."

Harrison leans in to Audrey and asks "How did she know they have hot cocoa and pretzels here?" ignoring the whole "Mr. Nicholas" part of the comment.

"I don't know. It is a Christmas store and maybe she just assumed that since hot cocoa is associated with Santa Claus they would have it."

"What about the pretzels then?"

After thinking about it, and taking the "Mr. Nicholas" part out of context to rationalize it she tells Harrison "Santa must have told her in their conversation that they have pretzels here. She was hungry before going to see him."

"Good point" agrees Harrison.

Looking at the wall just outside the entrance Audrey sees a letter board with a posted list of items that the snack area carries. "What they have is listed right here" she tells Heather.

Heather gives it a look. There is so much to choose from, but after a second, she tells her folks "I think I'll get a chocolate pudding..., milk..., and a slice of pepperoni pizza! That sounds good." She pauses for a moment before adding "Oh, and a Bosco Stick with ranch dressing!"

"Wow, you going to be able to eat all that and still have room for dinner later tonight?" asks Harrison.

"Sure! No problem!" exclaims Heather confidently. "Shopping always works up an appetite!"

"It does, doesn't it" Audrey chimes in laughing.

Shaking his head at the sheer nonsense of this, Harrison looks at them and says "Come on you two" and picks up a tray.

Making their way through the line, they pick up their desired meals. Harrison picks up a turkey sandwich, a piece of carrot cake, bag of chips, and Coke. Audrey, in the meantime keeps it simple, getting a good sized side salad and an ice tea. Heather sticks to exactly what she stated she wanted earlier, pudding, milk, slice of pepperoni pizza, and a Bosco stick with ranch dressing. Harrison ponies up for the bill while Heather and Audrey go find them a place to sit.

The seating area is rather full, and both Heather and Audrey scan to see if they can find a spot that will accommodate all three of them. Heather spots the perfect one after only a couple of moments and leads them right to it. It happens to be the same spot that Mr. Nicholas and she sat at earlier in the day. She decides that she will keep this little tidbit

to herself as she noticed that her folks didn't believe her story of her visit
with Mr. Nicholas.

4

Sitting down, Harrison pulls out a store directory map. As they eat,
the three of them discuss a shopping game plan for the remainder of the
afternoon. Harrison mentions that he would like to take a look at what
they have for lights in Section 15. Some of the strands they have for the
tree need to be replaced this year. He also says that he wouldn't mind
taking a look at the Christmas trees in the adjacent section. Audrey agrees
with him and adds she would like to take a look at the ornaments
throughout Section 10 and look at the Fontanini Nativity area in Section
5. Heather, of course, wants to look at everything. She rattles off at least
a half dozen or more things she wants to look at from Santas in Section 6,
to angels in Section 5, as well as other items in the various sections they
are going to along the way. It is going to be one exciting afternoon.

With their bellies now full and a plan somewhat in place, the family
makes their way back into the store, working their way into Section 10
first to look at the ornaments. Heather is amazed at how many different
types of ornaments there actually are here. They carry ornaments made of
spun glass, of various color, from countries near and far, and of every
shape, design, and theme anyone can possibly want.

The Christmas tree section is just as amazing. Trees of every shape,
size, even color all in this one section, which to her looks like a grand
forest. Some are lighted, others bare, so that you can put the lights on
yourself. She wonders how big a ladder her dad would need to decorate
the one they see that goes literally from floor to ceiling.

Over in Section 15, Harrison finds what he is looking for, and then they make their way back through the store to the Santas in Section 6 for Heather. Heather and her mother then spend quite a bit of time over in Section 5 looking at both the angels and the Fontanini Nativities. Both find things that they add to the cart.

After going through what they had planned to look at and shop for, they head back to the West Checkout to make their purchases. As they wait in line, Harrison is shocked at the time on his phone. Though it doesn't seem like they have shopped for very long, it has actually been hours.

"I can't believe the time" Harrison comments.

"Why, what time is it?" asks Audrey.

"It's well past 6 o'clock. And we still need to check into the lodge before going to dinner. Good thing I told them we would be arriving late."

"Good thing" agrees Audrey. "Also a good thing that a certain someone ate a big snack earlier or we'd be hearing it by now."

"What's for dinner?" chimes Heather.

"Spoke too soon there, Audrey" quips Harrison. Turning to Heather, he tells her "Well Sweetie, no visit to Bronner's and Frankenmuth is complete without getting an all-you-can-eat chicken dinner down at the Bavarian Inn."

"That sounds really good!" exclaims Heather as she goes to reach for the card Mr. Nicholas gave her. She stops short, hearing Mr. Nicholas's instructions echo in her mind...

> "When you get there, tell them Dorothy sent you and hand
> them this card. They will know what to do as it has all been
> arranged."

Audrey takes Heather to the side to help her get bundled up for leaving the store, while Harrison checks out. A few minutes later, he joins them, bags in hand. "So did you have a good day, Heather?" he asks.

"I sure did! I can't wait to come back!" she tells him.

"Glad to hear it" he tells her smiling. Taking his wife's arm and his daughter's hand, he walks them back into the West Entrance lobby area and out the doors onto the sidewalk outside the West Entrance.

Looking out, he sees the parking lot is spilling over with cars as far as the eye can see. Heather and Audrey get as wide eyed as Harrison at the sight as he jokes "Now here's the $25,000 question…does anyone remember where we parked?"

5

A light snow begins to fall as Harrison, Audrey and Heather meander down the sidewalk toward the parking lot. As they do Harrison and Audrey converse between themselves about who-what-when they did as they arrived so they can better discern where they parked upon arrival.

Heather, on the other hand, pays them no mind and really isn't that worried about it. In this particular moment, she is more caught up in the falling snow and how beautifully it glistens against the more than 100,000 colored Christmas lights that decorate the parking lot.

Harrison brings them to a halt upon reaching the seventy foot iconic Santa which is brilliantly lit by two ground spot lights. Heather watches as he puts his hand to his chin and begins talking to himself, all the while motioning to different areas they stopped by on the way in, to get somewhat of a bearing. She giggles to herself at the sight of this. Bronner's is a pretty amazing place. With all of the excitement, sights, and what she has experienced with Mr. Nicholas today, she is certain that *she* would've forgotten where the car was parked, just like her dad.

Taking her attention off her father, Heather looks up at the towering Santa before her. What happens next, she has to do a double take to make sure of what she sees.

The Santa winks at her.

She tugs at her mother's arm. "Mom…" she says faintly.

"Just a minute sweetheart" she replies as she tries to get the car finder app on her phone to come up.

Looking back up at the Santa, Heather watches as he slowly brings his hand from the position it is in holding his belt, to his lips, motioning for her to be still. He smiles as he does so. Heather nods slightly, acknowledging this. The Santa then motions for Heather to look into the parking lot as he points to a specific spot.

At first she doesn't catch what he is pointing at. Then she catches sight of it. On one of the light poles in the lot, a garland lighted star suddenly becomes brighter than all the rest in the lot. Blinking her eyes, she focuses her sight out in the lot just below it. Suddenly all the cars become transparent. The shape of each car is still apparent but since she can see through them it makes her task easier.

Looking up at the brightly lit garland star and peering through the transparent cars in the lot, she follows the pole down where she spies one that is out of place among the others. This one is solid, and it is theirs. Heather wheels around and looks back up at the Santa, gives him a wink, and then silently speaks the words *"Thank you"* to him.

The Santa smiles and nods, then returns to his designed position.

Without any warning, Heather grabs each of her parents' hands and exclaims "I KNOW WHERE WE PARKED! C, MON!"

She pulls them for only a moment before taking a quick glance to ensure they are following then darts into the parking lot heading right toward the spot she knows the car is parked.

"Heather! Come back here!" her mother yells to no avail. It is obvious the plea is falling on deaf ears. "Well, come on!" Audrey says to Harrison grabbing his arm, pulling him out toward the parking lot, "Don't just stand there like a bump on a log. She obviously remembers where we parked!"

They follow Heather down the long row of parked cars, which seems endless. Harrison notices as they go, she occasionally looks up, focusing on the brightened garland star. Heather is a good twenty-five feet in front of them when she comes to an immediate halt. Quickly she turns to see her folks catching up with her. "TAAA DAAA!" she chimes loudly, motioning to the car like one of "Barker's Babes" on the *Price Is Right*.

Harrison and Audrey finally catch up to Heather, both nearly out of breath. "Well I'll be" comments Harrison. "How did you all of a sudden remember where we had parked?" he asked.

Heather looked back toward the Santa standing in the spotlights, and giving her father a *"Cheshire Grin"* responds simply "Magic, Dad!"

"Magic, huh?" he questions shaking his head, knowing very well she knows something. "Okay, miss smarty pants. Get in the car now, will ya, so we can go check in and get something to eat."

"Yippee!!! Time for chicken!!!" she merrily screams while her dad unlocks the doors to the car for her and Audrey.

Once they are in and secure, Harrison shuts the doors and makes his way around the car, climbs in himself, and starts her up. After letting it warm he carefully backs out of the spot and heads toward the main drive. "How bout a quick tour around the building, so we can see all the decorations, before we leave?" he asks the two of them.

"Yeah!" says Heather. "I want to see them!"

"Okay by me" Audrey adds.

"Then let's take a tour, shall we?" says Harrison as he makes a left turn back around the store.

Slowly, Harrison drives around the complex allowing Heather to marvel at all the lights and displays that line the drive; an elf that leans on a sign that reads "North Pole"; a giant ornament that says "Merry CHRISTmas"; garland wrapped posts, some with stars, some with angels, others with candy canes and holly; Santas of all shapes and sizes; numerous Nativity décor; and a whole host of other Christmas themes. With so much to see, Heather is simply flabbergasted by it all.

Nearing the end of the drive, Heather sees the Silent Night Chapel. "Look…it's the Silent Night Chapel" she informs her parents asking "Isn't it beautiful?"

"Pretty impressive" comments Harrison.

"You're right, Heather. It is rather pretty" Audrey says.

Heather interjects "It's a replica of the actual chapel in Oberndorf, Austria where the song *"Stille Nacht"* or *"Silent Night"*, as we know it, was first sung in 1818. Mr. Bronner got permission from the Austrian government to build and replicate it here. You should see the inside of it. It's absolutely beautiful."

Harrison and Audrey once again are confused by her statements, yet amazed at the same time. Both thinking the same thing again, as good parents often do, Harrison gets it out first "Heather, how is it you know all of this?"

"Because I was there with Mr. Nicholas earlier, and he told me all about it" she answers without missing a beat, adding a little trivia to her response "Did you know it is *exactly* 230 steps from the South Entrance of Bronner's to the walkway of the chapel?"

"Must've missed that little tidbit of a fact" responds Harrison still confused. He thinks for a moment as they pulled up to Weiss Street. at the end of the driveway. After bringing the car to a stop, he looks into the back seat to check on Heather, to see that she is still enthralled with all the decorations. Looking over to Audrey he whispers *"How does she know all of this?"*

"I don't know" Audrey whispers back. *"She said that Mr. Nicholas told her about it. Maybe it was something she asked Santa about"*

"Possible. But how could she know what the inside looks like? We didn't even make it out there" he argues as he makes a right onto Weiss Street and makes the short trek out to South Main Street. Coming to a stop Harrison waits for traffic to clear so he can turn.

Audrey thinks for a second, not wanting to think of the notion that what Heather is saying is true, explains it away with a simple thought. *"Pamphlets"* she continues to whisper to Harrison so Heather can't hear. *"There are a bunch of pamphlets outside Santa's Workshop. Not to mention at the West Entrance as well. I know there is one in there on the chapel. I bet there are pictures of the inside in it."*

"That's got to be it" he agrees but not really believing it. He is starting to think that his daughter's rant earlier, when she got done visiting Santa, may have some truth to it. Regardless of this at the moment, he makes his way onto South Main Street to make the short trip down the road to the Bavarian Lodge where they where staying. The Bavarian Lodge is just up the hill from the Bavarian Inn where they will be going for dinner after they checked in.

As they pass back by Bronner's, Harrison and Audrey hear Heather say as it passes out of sight "Thank you, Mr. Wally Bronner. See you again soon."

The

Bavarian Inn

"Christmas is doing a little something extra for someone"

- Charles M. Schulz

Chapter 19

1

The trek down South Main Street is slow at best, and it has nothing to do with the 30 M.P.H. speed limits, either. Frankenmuth, (being one of the top Christmas towns in the United States) especially this time of the year, is bustling with visitors from both near and far. Though it must be driving her father nuts, the slow drive through town doesn't bother Heather one bit. It gives her plenty of time to take in and admire the Christmas decorations of the town which, coincidentally are as decked out as Bronner's.

Her attention is sidetracked from the Christmas décor when she hears the sound of familiar chimes coming from up ahead. Situating herself so she can see out the front window, she spots where the sound is coming from. Just ahead she sees the Glockenspiel tower, its many bells tolling while German figures dance around in unison. She is enchanted by the site of it. As enchanting as it is, it is what was located directly below the Glockenspiel that was more of an interest...the Bavarian Inn. A world famous restaurant known for its German specialties but better known for its Zehnder style, all-you-can-eat chicken dinners that have been a tradition since 1888. "*No visit to Frankenmuth is complete without one*" her father has said.

It takes her father a few light cycles, each feeling like an eternity, before he can make the turn onto Covered Bridge Lane, which leads up the driveway to the Bavarian Inn's parking lot. Coming to the three-way stop just beside the driveway, Harrison comments "We'll head up to the lodge and check in, then get settled and come back down for dinner. Sound good?"

"But dad, I'm hungry!" Heather complains.

"We'll eat after we check in, Heather. It won't take long" he assures her.

Audrey knows this is going to turn ugly quickly. An upset child is one thing. A *hungry*, upset child is something else. Before Heather can start complaining further she interjects "Didn't you say you told them we would be a late check-in?"

"Yes…" he says looking at Audrey, understanding the meaning in her eyes. "Yes, I did. Suppose we get something to eat and unwind from all of our shopping *before* we head up to check-in and call it a day."

"YES!" Heather belts out knowing she has pretty much gotten her way. She is very hungry, and that is a fact.

Turning into the small, packed lot, Harrison scans the lot for a place to park, which from the looks of things is going to be next to impossible. He also happens to notice that the wait for dinner is going to be a long one, as the line to get in stretches out the door. "Hope you all aren't really that hungry" he says.

"Why's that, dad?" asks Heather.

"Because we're going to have a wee bit of a wait, I'm afraid" pointing to the line. "Not to mention we have to find a place to park first."

Without missing a beat, Heather responds "No, we won't. I have connections."

"Really?" questions Audrey. "And whom might you know, young lady, that can hook us up?"

"You'll see" she remarks with a smile on her face, like a cat that just ate the canary.

"Well, Sweetie, your connections wouldn't happen to know of a good place to park so that we don't have to walk from Outer Mongolia?" asks Harrison smugly.

"Yeah, there's one right there, dad!" she states pointing at a spot that came suddenly out of nowhere and was just a few feet from the entrance.

Harrison hits the breaks hard, bringing the vehicle to a sudden, jerky stop so as not to overshoot it. He then backs up slightly to reposition himself and then pulls forward into the spot Heather has just pointed out.

"I gotcha covered, Dad! Called ahead for this primo parking spot for you" Heather cackles. It is a family joke when they find a spot that is exceedingly close to the entrance of wherever they may be going.

"Cute, smarty pants" he tells her as he puts the vehicle in park and turns off the engine.

"That's "*miss*" smarty pants, thank you! Small "m"" she retorts. Her tone and way in which she states it make her sound like a diva.

Harrison and Audrey laugh at how amusing this is, and Heather joins in knowing she has made a funny.

Exiting the car the family makes their way to the entrance. By this time the line has shrunken some and is now fully inside the building. Harrison opens the door, as any gentlemen would for a lady (or ladies in his case), allowing Audrey and Heather to enter first before following behind them.

2

They enter a small rotunda area with an interesting looking chandelier hanging directly from its center. A ledge, running around the lower end of the ceiling, is trimmed with various pines, carved woodland creatures, and lighted pine garland. Around the walls, there are a few comfortable chairs spaced proportionally for people to sit. The area itself has two distinctive paths...one that leads downstairs to the Castle Shop area of the establishment, the other leads up to the main dining area. This is the one they are most interested in.

It is a narrow corridor that is nothing more than a slowly inclining ramp. Its right side is lined with a line full of people anxiously waiting to eat. They all hug the wall leaving enough room to their left to allow others leaving or who have reservations, to pass. Being Heather knows they are of the latter category; she beckons her parents to follow.

"Heather, where do you think you are going? The line starts down here" her mother points out the obvious.

"But, Mom...I told you, I have connections" she insists once again. "C'mon!"

"Heather, listen to what your mother is saying. We just have to wait our turn like everyone else" Harrison explains.

"ARRRRGH!!!" she groans loudly, completely frustrated by her parents *not* listening to her. She knows fully well that she has a "connection". She just needs to find a way to show her parents what she is talking about. It isn't long before a solution presents itself.

Coming down the ramp, dressed in a traditional Dirndl dress of white and navy, wearing a red velvet hat with a dainty white feather, is a pretty young maiden with long blonde hair and rosy cheeks named Tammy.

Tammy makes her way down the line, offering the patrons drinks while they are waiting to be seated. Some take up the offer while others do not. Upon reaching Heather and her family, she does the same asking politely in an almost high pitched voice "Can I get you something to drink while you wait?"

Harrison looks over at Audrey then at Heather who both indicate that they are fine and will wait until they are seated. "No thank you" Harrison responds then adds "But we appreciate the offer."

"My pleasure" she politely responds.

Before she can leave Heather tugs on her arm, speaking up "Excuse me."

Tammy looks down at Heather and smiles. "Yes, li'l miss, what can I do for you?"

"I have an inquiry" says Heather, sounding very eloquent as she had been earlier in the day with Mr. Nicholas.

"Yes" responds Tammy.

Reaching into her pocket, Heather pulls out the card that Mr. Nicholas had given her before she departed his company. Handing it to Tammy she explains "I was instructed that when we arrived here, I was to let you know that Mrs. Dorothy sent me, and that I was to give someone this, and that everything had been arranged.

Taking the card from Heather, Tammy examines it closely. She smiles and kneels down to Heather's level. "You must be Heather. Am I correct?"

"Yes, I am. And these are my parents, Harrison and Audrey Fahs." she responds.

"We've been expecting you! It is very nice of you and your parents to join us for dinner this evening. If you will follow me, I'll get you taken care of right away.

"Dankeschon" (Thank you) Heather says to Tammy out of the blue, catching her parents off guard a bit.

Tammy, on the other hand, is rather impressed by this and responds by telling her "Bitteschon (You're welcome), Heather."

As Tammy leads them up the ramp, Heather looks back to her parents stating emphatically "I told you I had connections!"

Harrison and Audrey follow both speechless as to what just transpired, and both wondering the same thing…when did she learn to speak German, and where did she get that card?

3

The ramp is warmly and brightly lit by lamps that are adhered to the wall, that resemble lanterns, hang from the slanted ceiling. Along the walls are a variety of paintings of Bavaria, Germany and of the Frankenmuth area.

Heather marvels at it all as they reach the top of the ramp. Rounding the corner, the area becomes a bit more open as they approach a set of double doors that lead to a much larger waiting area. She observes that on either side of the door are numerous plaques and certificates that represent the many awards and recognitions that the Bavarian Inn has garnered over the years from all municipalities, local, state, and national.

While a hostess tends to those waiting on the right side, Tammy opens the left door and ushers Heather and her folks through. This area of the restaurant looks like what a traditional room in Bavaria would be like. The room is trimmed along the ceiling in ivy that is a deep green color, along with paintings, similar to those lining the ramp hallway, adorning the walls. As impressive as everything is, it is a picture that captures her attention the most. Slowly, Heather walks toward it, taking it in.

The picture is that of the Bavarian Inn's Zehnder Family, (one that shows the family beaming with joy and pride), though it is the lady positioned in the center of the photograph that is of particular interest to Heather. "Who is the lady in the center?" Heather asks Tammy.

"That is Mrs. Dorothy Zehnder, Heather. Her and her family are the proprietors of the Bavarian Inn, and a very good friend, I might add, of Mr. Nicholas."

"Is she here today?" asks Heather.

"The correct question, Heather, would be "when is she not here"? Mrs. Zehnder is a very dedicated lady. You will find her here at the inn, at least six days a week, cooking away in the kitchen as she is an excellent cook. She makes many of the items we serve and sell here at the Bavarian Inn. Now if you will follow me, I'll get you seated so you can eat some of her marvelous cooking."

Leading the way past the hostess stand, Tammy takes Heather and her parents into the Bavarian Room dining area. The room is vast, with lots of tables and booths made of wood and covered with white table linens with a runner of deep burgundy. The chairs that are placed at the tables are all handcrafted, with a Christmas tree design, cut out and centered, just below the top of the chair's back. Unique floral patterned carpeting covers the floor, bordered with solid green spots that seem to form a sort of walkway around the room. Fine china plates in handcrafted displays beautify the room, along with old photographs. What really sets this room apart from what Heather has seen so far are the rich, beautiful, detailed paintings on the wall, depicting such stories as *"Cinderella"*, *"Hansel and Gretel"*, *"Rapunzel"* and *"Snow White"* written by the well known German authors, The Brothers Grimm.

Tammy seats them at a nice little cozy table, just behind a wood partition inside the door. As the family remove their coats, sit down and get situated, she asks them "May I get your drink order started?"

"I would like an ice tea" quips Heather quickly. *"NO LEMON!"* she stresses to Tammy.

Tammy giggles at this as she jots it down on a pad that she had tucked into her apron. "And you, ma'am?" she asks looking to Audrey.

"An ice tea does sound really good" responds Audrey. Then adds "But I will take mine with lemon."

"E-W-W-W" sneers Heather.

"To each his own, young lady" says Harrison to her.

"And for you, sir?" asks Tammy.

"I'll take one of your good German-style beers. What would you recommend?" asks Harrison.

"Might I suggest the Hofbrau Original. It's a lager style that I think you'll enjoy."

"Sounds good to me. I'll take one of those, then" Harrison tells her.

"I will put these in, and your server will bring them out to you momentarily. Enjoy your dinner with us." Tammy then turns to Heather and tells her "It was a pleasure meeting you and your folks, Heather. Enjoy the rest of your stay with us."

"It was nice to meet you as well. Thank you" responds Heather as she watches Tammy take her leave to go put in their drink order.

4

As they wait for their drinks, Audrey and Harrison exchange looks. After an uncomfortable silence between them, Audrey breaks it by asking

Heather "Sweetie, where did you happen to get this card that gave you this "*connection*", as you call it, to accomplish this little feat?"

"You wouldn't believe me if I told you, just like earlier today" Heather snaps back defensively.

"That will do it with the attitude, young lady" Harrison quickly corrects her. "There has been a lot that has gone on today, Heather, which you've talked about or done that doesn't make much sense to us" he adds. "Yet, I'm sure there is a perfectly logical explanation for it all."

Heather hesitates as her parents give her the "*stare down*" as they wait for an answer. Knowing she isn't going to get out of this one, she gives in and tells them "The card was given to me as a gift from Mr. Nico…I mean Santa Claus. He told me to wait till we got here to present it. That's the truth!"

Both Harrison and Audrey look at Heather and can tell by the way she is acting, and the tone of her voice, that she isn't pulling the wool over their eyes. Looking at each other, they once again come to a conclusion that can't be farther from the truth. "Mom and Dad" they say in unison.

"Also, since when did you learn German?" asks Harrison.

She really didn't know. But rather than go into an explanation that her parents won't believe at this moment, she knows how to easily explain it. "I only know a couple of words, Dad. This is a German town, and there are expressions all over the place and what they mean. That's how."

Thinking about it for a moment, Harrison guesses this is very plausible reason. "Fair enough" he responds. "Now, since you have this "*connection*" with good ol' St. Nick, let's enjoy a nice world famous chicken dinner!"

5

At that same moment, a young waiter, dressed in a white shirt, lederhosen, thick wool sox, with dress shoes, and wearing a felt cap with a feather, sets down a stand and places a huge silver serving tray upon it.

"Good evening" he greets them with a German accent. "My name is Wilhelm, and I will be your server this evening." Getting himself situated Wilhelm, picks up the beer from the tray stating "Let's see here, the Hofbrau is for the gentleman, I presume."

"You are correct" states Harrison.

"Ah, then the ice teas must be for the ladies. Though I think the one with the lemon goes to mom, as the li'l miss isn't fond of them."

"You're good" Audrey tells him.

He nods in acknowledgment to them, and then continues "I have also brought out some bread and preserves for you to try. There are two kinds here. First there is Backofenbrot, which is a homemade white bread, and the other is called Stollen. This is bread made with fruit and nuts. Placing them on the table he then asks "Have we decided on dinner?"

"Yes, we have" replies Harrison. Turning to Heather he asks "Would you like to order for us all, Heather?"

"Sure! We would all like the family style chicken dinner, please!"

"An excellent and very popular choice, li'l miss! I'll have your soups and accompaniments out in just a couple of minutes. If there is anything else, please let me know."

"Thank you very much" replies Heather for all of them.

6

Over the next hour or so, they are treated to a most wonderful meal.
Wilhelm first brings out a dish of coleslaw, a bean salad, and a pasta salad
that has little chunks of ham and peas in it. Along with these come a
cranberry relish and noodle soup with crackers for each of them.

Being the picky eater that she is, Heather stays clear of most of it,
letting her parents have at it. She does, however, down her noodle soup
without any hassle or complaint. She enjoys it so much that she asks for
seconds while eating some of the white bread.

When they are ready, Wilhelm brings out the main course: mashed
potatoes, mashed to perfection, a bowl of thick chicken gravy, dressing, a
vegetable du jour, buttered noodles with a crumb topping, and most
importantly, what they had come to the Bavarian Inn for in the first place,
a large platter of the world famous Zehnder-style chicken. Heather and
her parents watch and wait patiently as Wilhelm places the food upon the
table in a very specific fashion. When finished he asks "Is there anything
else I can bring you at the moment?"

"No, I think that will do it for the moment" Harrison responds.
"Thank you."

"Not a problem, sir" replies Wilhelm. "I'll be by to check on you in a
few" he states and then takes his leave from them.

For a brief moment they all sit there in silence, taking in the vast meal
that was just placed before them. Heather can't believe how much there
is. To her, it is just like being at her grandparent's house for a big Sunday
meal or a holiday dinner. Where to begin is her next question. Audrey
breaks the silence by telling them all "Well don't just sit there and let it get
cold…dig in!"

Without further hesitation, they all begin to fill their plates and enjoy the meal before them. Audrey sticks with just a single helping of everything, while Harrison loads up twice on the chicken, potatoes, gravy, and dressing. Heather, on the other hand, eats quite a bit of chicken, some mashed potatoes and gravy, and pretty much devours the entire bowl of buttered noodles on her own. The entire family eats their fill, even managing to save room for dessert, which Wilhelm brings to them when they have finished with the main meal.

Dessert is a small dish of homemade ice cream of vanilla, chocolate, or cranberry for each person and is accompanied with a small plate of gingerbread and molasses cookies for all to share. Harrison goes for the chocolate, Audrey decides the cranberry sounded good, and Heather goes for the vanilla. When Wilhelm returns with their selections, each has a little Bavarian figure sticking out of the top of the ice cream: a Bavarian lad for Harrison while both Audrey and Heather have Bavarian ladies in theirs. They enjoy the dessert as much as they did the dinner, with Heather hoarding as many of the cookies as her parents would allow her to.

Upon completion of dessert Harrison motions for Wilhelm. As he reaches the table asks "Would you kindly bring us a couple of boxes so that we can take some of this home with us?"

"Of course, sir" replies Wilhelm. "Is there anything else I can do for you this evening?"

"Other than the check, I think we're set, thanks."

"There is no check, sir" says Wilhelm.

"What do you mean there is no check?" asks Harrison.

"The card that the young lady presented earlier has taken care of everything" explains Wilhelm, a fact that Heather already knows.

"Okay, then. That is an awful nice gift Santa gave us. Guess we'll just have to thank him when we see him next. Thank you for everything, Wilhelm."

"It was my pleasure. You all have a good evening and a Merry Christmas. Hope that you'll come visit us again" says Wilhelm, then goes to get the boxes as requested.

They sit there silently until Wilhelm returns with the boxes. Audrey then boxes the leftovers up neatly and places them in the small bag that Wilhelm also brought with them. As she does this Harrison asks "So shall we head up to the lodge and call it a day?"

"Sounds good to me" states Audrey. "I don't know about the rest of you, but I am bushed! What about you, Heather?"

"I'm good. But I think I ate way too much, so you may have roll me out the door and out to the car!"

Harrison and Audrey break out in a hearty laugh at this statement.

Putting their coats on, the family heads out from the dinning area back into the main lobby. Coming upon the door through which they entered, Heather catches a glimpse of Mr. Nicholas heading down the ramp and rushes after him.

7

"HEATHER! SLOW IT DOWN!" Audrey yells as Harrison and she rush after her.

They catch up with Heather near the bottom of the ramp where she has come to a halt. She stands in front of her…Mr. Nicholas.

Before her parents can scold her, or even get a word out, she motions for them to be quiet and points to Mr. Nicholas, who stands conversing with a young boy (who might be the whole sum of eight, perhaps nine at best), with a slight attitude to boot. They listen as the young boy peppers Mr. Nicholas with a variety of questions.

"If you are who you say you are" the boy suggests, "Then where you born?"

"I was born in a little village called Patara" Mr. Nicholas responds. "It is a small village in what is now modern day Turkey."

"Okay. Were you at the first council of Bishops?"

"Yes, I was. It was held in Nicea. There we discussed many things and where I helped to write what you would know as "*The Apostle's Creed*"."

"When did you pass, and what is that day known as today?"

"I passed on December the 6th, and it known today as St. Nicholas Day."

The young boy continues with a barrage of other questions. Upon hearing all the answers he extends his hand to Mr. Nicholas and states with all certainty "Put 'er there! You are who you say you are. It is a pleasure to meet you, St. Nicholas."

Mr. Nicholas shakes the young boy's hand replying "The pleasure is mine" then watches the young boy scamper back to his parents who are waiting. Looking up, his gaze catches that of Heather's and he smiles as only St. Nicholas can.

"Mr. Nicholas!" screams Heather and rushes over to him giving him a big hug.

"Good to see you again, Heather. I trust you and your family enjoyed your dinner here this evening?"

"We sure did! It was delicious! And, thank you, again for it!"

"You are most welcome. These must be your parents" he states, looking back at Harrison and Audrey, who stand there just a bit confused at the situation.

"I'm sorry. My manners" she replies motioning for her mom and dad to come over. As they do, she says "Mom and Dad, this is Mr. Nicholas. He's the one who showed me today how he really became Santa and what Christmas is truly all about. He is also the one who took care of dinner this evening for us all. You wanted to thank Santa, Dad, the next time you saw him you said. So here he is!"

Nicolas extends his hand telling them "It is a pleasure to meet you, Harrison, and you as well, Audrey. You have a wonderful young daughter and should be very proud of her."

Shaking his hand, confused at how he knows their names, Harrison asks "You're the Santa from Bronner's?"

"Yes I am" Nicholas responds.

"And it was *you* who gave our daughter the card for the dinner this evening?"

"Just as she told you" says Nicholas.

Harrison and Audrey give each other a perplexed look trying to figure this one out. Seeing this Nicholas says "You thought it was your parents who gave Heather the card and set up dinner for this evening."

"Yes, I did…but wait a second…how could you know that?!" questions Harrison.

"Because he is Santa Claus!" says Heather stating the obvious, which escapes both of her parents.

Giving a hearty chuckle, as only Santa Claus can, he says to Harrison and Audrey "Your daughter speaks the truth. I am Santa Claus, or St. Nicholas if you will just as the young lad knew and Heather learned today. Look into my eyes" he tells them.

Both Harrison and Audrey gaze deeply into Nicholas's endearing eyes. Being Santa Claus derives his strength and abilities from God himself, he is able to reach deep within a person's soul and find that little piece inside that makes them a child at any age, and in that, shows them the magic and truth of it all.

Nicholas breaks his gaze, and in doing so, it becomes clear to them both. Heather did indeed have all this knowledge because she truly had experienced it all. Everything that she had said and done today, and they had trounced away as something else, was in fact true. Leaning down to Heather, they hug her tightly and express their apologies for not believing her or taking her seriously, which she accepts with humility.

Zehnder's

Wooden Bridge

Home

"Christmas is forever, not just for one day, for loving, sharing, giving, are not to put away like bells and lights and tinsel, in some box up a shelf."

- *Norman Wesley Brooks*
"Let Everyday Be Christmas"
(1976)

Chapter 20

1

"Edelweiss" begins to chime from the bells of the Glockenspiel. It is one of those familiar tunes that one would recognize from one of two places, either from the Roger and Hammerstein's *"The Sound Of Music"*, or more likely from the Benediction during a Sunday morning church service. After a short interlude of the song, the bells begin to toll the hour.

It is the tolling which catches Nicholas's keen ear. Casually, he retrieves his watch from his breast pocket, confirming the time in accordance to the final toll of the bells. Replacing the watch into his pocket, he respectfully announces "Well, my friends, the hour grows late. It is time for me to be on my way."

Harrison gives his watch a glance seeing that it is past 9 o'clock "It *is* getting late" he concurs with Nicholas. "And we still need to check into the lodge before we can get settled for the remainder of the evening." He looks to Heather and adds "Not to mention it's past someone's bedtime, and with all the fun and excitement of the day, she should be getting some rest, don't you think?"

"A-w-w, Dad!" whines Heather. "I'm not even t-i-i-r-r-ed" she states while trying to fight back a yawn.

Nicholas notices this and tells her "I think I have to agree with your father, Heather. You have had quite the day. Not to mention that since you are staying up at the lodge, at this time of night, Judith Zehnder Keller would tell you *"It's sleepy time in Frankenmuth"."*

"Oh, alright" she says giving in reluctantly knowing this is one argument she cannot win. She begrudgingly leads them all out the door and into the parking lot.

2

As they reach the end of the sidewalk, Heather turns to Mr. Nicholas and asks "So, Mr. Nicholas, where are you parked? We got lucky and got a spot right up close" she tells him pointing to their car just a few feet away.

"That *is* really close" he agrees. "Called ahead for your dad to get him that primo parking spot did you" he says repeating her words of earlier to her father.

"Sure did!"

"I'd say you have a little magic in you to pull off such a feat. But to answer your inquiry as to where I parked, I didn't drive here. I am meeting an acquaintance of mine up by Zehnder's Holz Brucke in a couple of minutes."

"Zehnder's who sees rug?" not understanding the pronunciation of the words Nicholas just spoke.

"No it's holzes brugge" says Nicholas enunciating it. "It means wooden bridge in German."

"A wooden bridge?" comments Audrey. "Not something you see bridges made of these days. It's so narrow, and to me, looks a little scary from what I saw as we were driving in."

"Nonsense!" states Nicholas. "We have many bridges like this over in Bavaria, where I reside. They may look scary, but they are as solid as they come. This one here was built using the same style framing techniques and solid craftsmanship that built ones where I live, only using more modern techniques."

"So it is safe then?" asks Heather.

"Safe and very sound, I assure you. It took them two years to build when Tiny, that would be Mr. Zehnder, Dorothy's husband, had it commissioned. It's made from very solid, sturdy wooden planks from Douglas fir trees. You would call them Christmas trees."

"It's made from Christmas trees?!" Heather says astoundingly.

"Yes, it is" Mr. Nicholas tells her reassuringly.

Convinced by this, she turns to her mother and confidently tells her "Then we have nothing to worry about."

"That settles it then" says Harrison as he walks up to Nicholas, extending his hand. "Thank you, Nicholas, for everything you have done today. It's very much appreciated."

"It was my pleasure, Harrison" responds Nicholas shaking Harrison's hand. He then turns to Audrey telling her "You have a wonderful daughter, Audrey. Thank you for allowing her to share my knowledge on this day."

"You're welcome. Thank you again, as well, for everything."

"Again, it was my pleasure" responds Nicholas as he now turns to Heather. She stands there, tears in her eyes ready to lose it, when he kneels down to her. She goes to tell him goodbye, but is stopped mid-word by him putting a finger to her lips. "Where I live Heather, we do not say goodbye. We say auf wiedershen."

"Auf wiedershen?" questions Heather repeating it with perfect German enunciation. "What does it mean?"

Nicholas explains to her "What auf wiedershen actually means in German is "until I see you again". And I know for certain, as certain as you and I are talking right here and now, we will see each other again one day."

Knowing full well Mr. Nicholas speaks the truth, this perks Heather right up. Drying her eyes, Heather composes herself, looks at him confidently and tells him "Auf weidershen!" before lunging at him to give him an enormous hug.

Nicholas returns the hug as her parent's smile, Audrey almost in tears at the joy she sees playing out before her. "Auf wiedershen, Heather. You and your family have a very Merry Christmas, and remember the true reason for the season."

"I will never forget, Mr. Nicholas. Ever. Merry Christmas to you as well" she tells him as she takes her mother's outstretched hand and heads out to their car.

Nicholas strolls casually up towards Zehnder's Holz Brucke and observes the family secure themselves in their vehicle, back out of the parking spot and get underway, making their way as well up to the bridge.

3

While Heather and her family slowly make their way through the small parking lot in front of the Bavarian Inn, Nicholas moves swiftly up the hill to Zehnder's Holz Brucke. Reaching the crest, he sees a cloaked figure standing near the bridge's walkway, gazing into the clear, moonlit sky. The moon softly glistens off the waters of the Cass River that runs below.

The Cloaked Gentleman waits until Nicholas is just a few feet from Him. "A beautiful silent night" He states before asking "Wouldn't you agree, Nicholas?"

"I do concur, Lord" knowing the voice of the Cloaked Gentleman well. "It is a very beautiful, silent night. A light snow would further enhance its beauty. If I might make that suggestion" says Nicholas.

Removing His hood, the Lord turns to him. Surveying the night sky and surroundings He responds "So it would, old friend." The Lord no more than finishes his agreement with Nicholas, when a light snow begins to fall. "Perfect" He simply states smiling. He then nods to Nicholas, who turns to see Heather and her parents slow as they pass them by.

Heather quickly rolls down her window so as not to miss the opportunity to see and speak to Mr. Nicholas one last time. "Thanks again, Mr. Nicholas! I had a great day and Merry Christmas! Auf Wiedershen!!!" she yells from the car. Before sitting back and rolling up her window, she recognizes the Lord who stands next to Nicholas. As she goes to speak, she is stopped short by the Lord motioning quiet, knowing her parents have had quite the day with their daughter with everything. She nods in acknowledgment, and clasping her hands in a praying fashion bows her head and silently mouths *"Thank you."*

"You're welcome" she hears in her thoughts from the Lord as she rolls up her window.

The Lord and Nicholas watch as the family crosses over the bridge, then turn to the left before disappearing from view as they head to the Bavarian Lodge to call it a night.

4

"You did a fine job today, Nicholas. Just as I knew you would" says the Lord.

Bowing in reverence, Nicholas responds "Thank you, Lord." He pauses for a slight moment before stating "I understood why You chose her over the course of our visit. She is a remarkable child."

"Yes, she is" the Lord acknowledges. "The mind of a child is truly amazing. Nurture them, give them solid values, some perhaps old fashioned, some traditions, and oh the change they can make in this world. Much as you did, Nicholas, and that you still do to this day."

"All one has to do is believe and have faith, and anything is possible. Heather is proof of this as You already knew."

"As are the others you touched today, Nicholas. Her parents…even the young boy who wanted to do the twenty questions routine." Looking around, the Lord admires the small town of Frankenmuth before telling Nicholas "It is always a slow process, my friend. But in time all shall be as it should be."

"It was a pleasure as always to serve You, Lord. I am always at Your service" states Nicholas in full faith.

The Lord places a hand upon Nicholas's shoulder. Nicholas bows humbly as he does, and is told by the Lord "It is always appreciated. The bridge will take you home as I take my leave of you."

As Nicholas brings his head up, he sees that the Lord has gone, with not as much as a footprint to prove He was there. All that remains is simply a silent night.

5

Nicholas strolls over to the edge of the sidewalk near the entry to the bridge from the Bavarian Inn side and nonchalantly peers down toward the opposite end. His keen observation shows him that not even a mouse stirs at the other end. Turning his head to the opposite direction, he takes a gander down Covered Bridge Lane to witness a lot of hustling and bustling on Main Street of all who have come to visit. Though there is a plethora of activity going on down the way, nothing at that particular moment, be it car or person, is coming his way.

Content that all is well, he steps from the sidewalk down onto the road. The moment his foot hits the asphalt of the road, everything around him seems to slow and come to a complete standstill, as if time has been frozen.

Slowly, Nicholas begins his trek across Zehnder's Holt Brucke. As he strolls, he admires the beautiful craftsmanship that was put into this bridge. His well-honed senses pick up the faint remnants of the smell of pine from the Douglas firs used in crafting the bridge, and the crisp smells of Christmas on the air that are so nostalgic and reminiscent of the smells around his dwelling within the Bavarian Forest. It is with this thought that Nicholas realizes that he is halfway there. Laying a finger aside of his nose, he gives the slightest of nods towards the exit ahead.

The scenery that is Frankenmuth, Michigan's Little Bavaria begins to blur and twist as an aperture opens. Once fully open, what lies before him becomes crystal clear. Walking out of the bridge, Nicholas enters the clearing within the Bavarian Forest that lies just in front of his home. Taking a deep breath he breaths in the cool crisp air of the forest. He turns to watch the aperture close behind him, sealing off the scenery of

Frankenmuth, reverting it back to that of the vast forest he so knows and has come to admire.

Smiling, Nicholas stands there for a moment, taking it all in, thinking how his life and his new friend Heather's have been enhanced today by God's grace. If only everyone will take the Lord into their hearts, as he had, and be animated by the Holy Spirit, then the Spirit of Christmas will live in everyone, not just once a year, but all year through. One day it will happen. Until then he will continue doing the Lord's work, giving of himself as he has done all these centuries and beyond, as long as he is needed. But for now, it is time for rest. Leisurely, he makes his way toward his cottage ready, to settle in for the night.

A bright star, shimmering brightly in the clear, night sky shows him the way.

THE END

Author's
Note

"He who has not Christmas in his heart will never find it under the tree."

- Roy L. Smith

"Unless we make Christmas an occasion to share our blessings, all the snow in Alaska won't make it 'white'."

- Bing Crosby

Author's Note

Myth, legend, an actual person, he is each and all. He goes by many names throughout the world depending upon the country you happen to reside in. Kris Kringle, Pere Noel, Weihnactsmann, Babbo Natale, Grandfather Frost, Sinterklaas, and Father Christmas...all names for the jolly old man in the bright red suit that we all grew up knowing simply as Santa Claus. Although I'm a grown adult, I can tell you without any hesitation or trepidation that I still believe in Santa Claus to this day.

One might chuckle at the notion but suffice it to say Santa Claus was always a "part" of the Christmas Season for me while I was growing up. It wasn't until I was older that I began to realize how much he really is a true personification of the season itself. Allow me to illustrate.

There has always been a magical quality that is associated with the Christmas Season. Santa is that magic. It's a season of giving to others. Santa Claus is a known as a gift-giver. Then the most important aspect of the season itself is it has a distinct "spirit" about it. Santa's essence is none other than the "Spirit of Christmas" and it radiates the values of the season...Peace (The Spirit of the Season), Hope (The Joy of the Season), Love (The Heart of the Season) and Joy (The Reason for the Season...The Birth of Our Lord and Savior, Jesus Christ).

Dig into it even more and you'll find the traits which lie within Santa Claus aren't there by mistake, they're intentional. Intentional as they were modeled after the same attributes of a third century bishop we know as St. Nicholas. St. Nicholas may not have had the magic per se of Santa Claus, but his magic was his undying faith in God. He too, was a giver. It is a matter of fact that he gave selflessly of himself to all those in need: the poor, the destitute, and the down trodden. Finally, St. Nicholas's spirit was animated by the "Holy Spirit" itself. This is one and the same as "Spirit of Christmas"; and he radiated Peace, Hope, and Love, those "Fruits of the Holy Spirit" throughout his entire life. His Joy was his love of his Savior, Jesus Christ.

I mentioned earlier that Santa Claus was a "part" of the Christmas Season for me. That was always the true intention of Santa Claus, to be part of the season, not the reason for it. Unfortunately, many of us have lost sight of what the real reason for the season is, that being the celebration of the Birth of Our Savior, Jesus Christ. Even if you're not a religious person, and don't want to look at it from that point of view, then look at it from the perspective that the Christmas Season is also about family, traditions, and giving to others. If you hold either true to your heart, then I believe what I've watch erode away as I've gotten older will eventually restore itself to what the Christmas Season truly was meant to be.

Speaking of others, this novel wouldn't be possible without thanking the following…

For starters, I can't begin to thank enough the late Wally Bronner and the Bronner Family for creating the beautiful store of Bronner's CHRISTmas Wonderland. Your establishment is amazing and inspirational in so many ways. Each and every time that I visit, it is as though I've come home and am at peace. It's difficult to explain. There is no doubt in my mind though that the Spirit of Christmas (The Holy Spirit), the same one which animated and was at the center of both St. Nicholas's and Wally Bronner's life, resides there without fail 365. Your store's motto says it so beautifully and eloquently…

"Enjoy CHRISTmas, It's His Birthday; Enjoy Life, It's His Way."

Father Joseph Marquis...Your annual program you present at

Bronner's CHRISTmas Wonderland of *"From Saint To Santa: How Saint*

Nicholas Became Santa Claus", is one of the many inspirations for this story.

From the first time I saw it, and each and every time I've seen it since, I'm

truly fascinated by how it conveys a wealth of information and insight in

such a way that people, no matter the age, benefit from. I've picked up

something new each time and every time I see it, and it's magnificent!

Thank you very much for allowing me to use it within my story. I also

have to thank you, once again, for taking the time to meet with me on that

November evening back in 2013. Imparting your wisdom, knowledge,

and first hand experience with St. Nicholas to me was uplifting and

inspirational in ways that I can't even begin to explain. It was something

that I will never forget. It was because of this meeting that the final piece

of the puzzle I was seeking was put in place, affirming to me that I was on

the proper path. In the Spirit of Saint Nicholas I thank you, my friend for

all that you've contributed to my project, your continued support, and

most of all for your friendship. It is much appreciated.

Many thanks to Dorothy Zehnder and the Zehnder Family for their

World Famous Chicken Dinners at the Bavarian Inn Restaurant that I

have had the pleasure to enjoy each and every time I have visited

Frankenmuth. Your staff is always top notch and the food always

fantastic. I look forward to dining there each and every time I visit

Frankenmuth. As I stated in the story, no visit to Frankenmuth is

complete without a Zehnder's World Famous Chicken Dinner!

Speaking of Frankenmuth, also known as Michigan's Little Bavaria,

there's just something about your town that I seem to have a connection

with. I would say that it has to do with the fact that it reminds of Reed

City, Michigan, where my grandparents lived. Yours is a town built on faith, family, and traditions; are some things that I feel have been greatly lost in the world today. Thanks for keeping such things of value. You are my home away from home.

A very special thank you needs to be given to Alda Monteschio for writing the beautiful poem of *"Santa's Christmas Prayer".* I found this poem while doing research for *"Saint Nick"* and I was amazed on how well it spoke about the story I was writing. I want you to know how much I appreciate you allowing me to use it to start off my story.

Kudos to Biggby Coffee Plainfield, Grand Rapids, Michigan as this third book was written and edited here. I have officially dubbed your establishment as my official "office" in which to work. Thank you for providing a delightful atmosphere in which to write, not to mention excellent coffees (such as Vanilla Beans made with soy, Butter Bears and Ice Teas) to name just a few of my favorites, and bragels to enjoy while doing my work. Special thanks to baristas Rebekah, Kenzie, and Leanne. You ladies make my "Writing Wednesdays" and all my other "office" visits absolutely fantastic with your kindness and great customer service. Keep up the great work, ladies! It is appreciated more than you know.

Though Biggby Coffee Plainfield is and always will be my primary "office" of choice in which to work from, I would be remiss not to mention and give thanks to a small, little independent coffee house in Hudsonville, Michigan by the name of Mocha & Music. Mocha & Music served me as a secondary "office" in which to work from during a time when my wife and I were sharing a car. I was saddened to learn that they closed their doors for the last time on October 5, 2013. Thanks for a uniquely different atmosphere to work in and some really good cappuccinos to enjoy while doing so. You will be missed.

Best selling authors, like Stephen King, have professional editors at their disposal to ensure silly little mistakes don't make it into their works.

Though I'm not yet a best selling author, I say who needs a professional editor?! I know someone who is a much better deterrent to such things. Her name is Hazel Benedict, alias Helen with the blood red pen. If she can point out multiple mistakes in the work of a best selling author, whose professional editor and another author missed, then there's no doubt she found my many mistakes with ease. Am I in the past or in the present? With your help, and humor, you've kept me in the right time I need to be in. Thank you for being a great reader and a fantastic editor for me on this book. You're always making sure I'm looking my best!

For my friends the "Goonies"…Aaron Sanford, Tammy Foster, Julie Jenison, Richard Goebel, Jeff Van't Hof, and Lisa Wierckz…You've all stuck with me through thick and thin since the day we first met each other. I am truly blessed and honored for your friendship and to have you all in my life. I thank you all for your support and encouragement, as it means the world to me.

To my "Guardian Angels", Royce Saunders (Grandfather), Eithel Saunders (Grandmother), and most of all, Carolynn Califf (Mother), for instilling within me my faith, love, and values of Christmas that you all held so dear. It's because of you, I hold Christmas in my heart with such high esteem. I will continue to hold Christmas in my heart now and forever, as each of you did, and promise it will be passed on.

When I started this novel, you were my girlfriend. Then as the story progressed, we became engaged. Finally, as the story came to an end, you became my wife. You made me the happiest man on the planet that day, Angela Kroupa. It is the proudest moment of my life and one that I will never forget and will always cherish. Thank you for all of your love, support, and for always being my rock. I don't know what I would do without you in my life.

Finally, to you the reader, I hope that you've enjoyed this story as much as I enjoyed telling it. I thank you for your support!

I leave you now with one final acknowledgement...to St. Nicholas and this prayer that is said in his honor...

"We call upon Your mercy, O Lord
Through the intercession of St. Nicholas
Keep us safe amid all dangers
So that we may go forward
Without hindrance on the road of salvation."
Amen.

Brandon G. Kroupa
Grand Rapids, Michigan
September 2015

Information Sources

"Fröhliche Weihnachten und einen guten Rutsch ins neue Jahr!"

Translation:
"Merry Christmas and a good slip into the New Year!"

- German Holiday Greeting

Sources Of Information

Ideas for stories come from the imagination. They are inspired to fruition by our own experiences, perhaps a song or a quote, a picture or scene, a place, even by Divine influence. At times these stories need a tad bit of help from actual facts and the knowledge of others. This aids the author in telling the story to its fullest potential while at the same time making it seem realistic and plausible. I can say with certainty that this story would not be what it is without the help of the knowledge I learned from these sources.

The primary sources of information for this novel, used throughout its entirety, were provided by the following…

- St. Nicholas Center: Discovering The Truth About Santa Claus, www.stnicholascenter.org, April 13, 2008 and May 18, 2008.

- Bronner's CHRISTmas Wonderland, www.bronners.com.

- Father Joseph Marquis, Executive Director of the Saint Nicholas Institute, www.stnicholasintitute.org.

- Frankenmuth Chamber of Commerce, "Frankenmuth…Michigan's Little Bavaria" 2015 Official Visitor's Guide, www.frankenmuth.org, 2015.

- "*Santa's Christmas Prayer*" by Alda Monteschio, Copyright 2001-2015 Alda Monteschio – All Rights Reserved. Used By Permission.

Other sources of information that aided in the writing of this novel were provided by…

Chapter 1:

- Zell, www.wikipedia.org, June 26, 2012.

- Zell-Bayericher-Wald JPG Photo, commons.m.wikimedia.org, Use granted under the terms of GNU Free Documentation License, February 23, 2015.

Chapter 2:

- Bavarian Forest, www.wikipedia.org, June 26, 2012.

Chapter 4:

- Bronner's CHRISTmas Wonderland, "20 C+M+B_ _", Flyer.

Chapter 7:

- Yes, Virginia, there is a Santa Claus, www.newseum.org/yesvirgina/, November 10, 2008.

- Virginia O'Hanlon Photo c.1897 (Courtesy of James Temple), www.newseum.org/yesvirginia/photogallery, November 10, 2008.

- Editorial Writer Frances P. Church Photo (The Century Archives Foundation), www.newseum.org/yesvirginia/photogalley, November 10, 2008.

Chapter 8:

- Good News Publishers, "A CHRISTmas Story: The Story Of Wally Bronner" Pamphlet, 2009.

- Bronner's CHRISTmas Wonderland, "Annual Tidings 2008" Pamphlet, 2009.

- Bavarian Inn Lodge, "Bronner Family", www.bavarianinn.com/familyhistory, December 2014.

Chapter 10:

- Father Joseph Marquis, "From Saint To Santa: How St. Nicholas Became Santa Claus", Recorded Program From November 9, 2013, Used By Permission.

Chapter 11:

- Hallmark Cards, Inc., "The Legend Of Santa Claus", Hallmark Keepsake Ornaments Jubilee Edition, 2001.

- Dr. Richard P. Bucher, "The Origin of Santa Claus and the Christian Response to Him", Our Redeemer Lutheran Church, www.orlutheran.com, June 25, 2012.

Chapter 12:

- Pastor Joseph Mohr and Franz Xaver Gruber, "Silent Night (Stille Nacht)", 1818.

- Bronner's CHRISmas Wonderland, "Silent Night Memorial Chapel" Pamphlet, August 2006.

- Good News Publishers, "The Story Of Silent Night" Pamphlet, 1999.

Chapter 14:

- William J. Federer, "There Really Is A Santa Claus – "The History Of Saint Nicholas & Christmas Holiday Traditions", pg. 35, 2003.

Chapter 15:

- Author Unknown, "God Rest Ye Merry, Gentlemen" (Traditional English Christmas Carol, Mid 18th Century), Published in 1833 by William B. Sandys.

Chapter 19:

- Bavarian Inn Restaurant, "Bavarian Inn Restaurant, World Famous Restaurant, Frankenmuth, Michigan" Pamphlets, 2013 & 2014.

- Bavarian Inn Restaurant, "Dinner Menu", November 2014.

- Bavarian Inn Lodge, "Zehnder Family", www.bavarianinn.com/familyhistory, December 2014.

- Father Joseph Marquis, Meeting on November 9, 2013 at Frankenmuth McDonald's.

Chapter 20:

- Zehnder's Holz Brucke (Wooden Bridge), www.my.net-link.net, December 10, 2014

Photos:

- All photos for the Chapter Covers in this novel, except Chapters 1, 6, 7, and noted above, where taken by the author, Brandon G. Kroupa, at Bronner's CHRISTmas Wonderland and The Bavarian Inn. (November 2012 to June 2015)

- Cover Photo *"Father Christmas Looking At Snow Falling Onto His Hand"* #8436117 Courtesy of istock.com/Dean Mitchell. Used By Permission per the istock.com Standard License Agreement.

THANK YOU